YOUNG MAN'S WAR

CASTALIA HOUSE

SCIENCE FICTION
Superluminary by John C. Wright
City Beyond Time by John C. Wright
Back From the Dead by Rolf Nelson
Mutiny in Space by Rod Walker
Alien Game by Rod Walker
Young Man's War by Rod Walker

MILITARY SCIENCE FICTION
There Will Be War Volumes I and II ed. Jerry Pournelle
Starship Liberator by David VanDyke and B. V. Larson
Battleship Indomitable by David VanDyke and B. V. Larson
The Eden Plague by David VanDyke
Reaper's Run by David VanDyke
Skull's Shadows by David VanDyke

FANTASY
Summa Elvetica by Vox Day
A Throne of Bones by Vox Day
A Sea of Skulls by Vox Day
The Green Knight's Squire by John C. Wright
Iron Chamber of Memory by John C. Wright
Awake in the Night by John C. Wright

FICTION
An Equation of Almost Infinite Complexity by J. Mulrooney
The Missionaries by Owen Stanley
The Promethean by Owen Stanley
Brings the Lightning by Peter Grant
Rocky Mountain Retribution by Peter Grant
Hitler in Hell by Martin van Creveld

NON-FICTION
SJWs Always Lie by Vox Day
SJWs Always Double Down by Vox Day
The LawDog Files by LawDog
The LawDog Files: African Adventures by LawDog
Equality: The Impossible Quest by Martin van Creveld
A History of Strategy by Martin van Creveld

YOUNG MAN'S WAR

ROD WALKER

CASTALIA HOUSE

Young Man's War

Rod Walker

Published by Castalia House
Tampere, Finland
www.castaliahouse.com

Cover: Lars Braad Andersen
Editor: Vox Day

ISBN: 978-952-7065-63-1

Contents

Chapter 1

Invasion Day

My dad had problems, and that's the only reason my sister and I are still alive.

It's weird to think about what life was like before Invasion Day. It's kind of like remembering a dream, but the sort of dream you have when you're sick with a bad fever. I remember the kinds of things people used to worry about back then, and now it all seems insane. Nobody was starving, everyone had the latest tech, yet everyone was angry about stupid stuff floating around the Internet. People argued about what one celebrity had said about another celebrity, and which singer was dating what actress, and what sports star was demanding too much money, and about the latest twists and turns in their favorite television series.

A lot of things changed after Invasion Day.

General Culver says that everyone has their own Invasion Day story, and they're always sad, and he's right about that. He also says their stories are ultimately hopeful, even though they're awful, because the people telling them survived and weren't slaughtered, converted into zombies, or devoured by the Dark. I'm not sure if he's right about that.

Anyway, the only reason that my sister and I survived Invasion Day was because of my father.

His name was Daniel Kane, and he was a sergeant in the Chicago Police Department. Dad wasn't the kind of cop who gave talks at schools or helped old ladies across the street. I've heard some stories from people who knew him, and apparently he once shot a suspect's dog in front of the suspect's children in order to coerce a confession… and the man turned out to be innocent. Another time someone tried recording him beating a suspect, and Dad responded by shattering the man's cell phone and beating him to a pulp.

The man later testified that he had tripped and fallen off the curb.

No one ever messed with Daniel Kane.

Not twice, anyway.

So I don't think my father was a good man. At the time, I thought it was normal, but later I realized it was kind of like getting raised by a Mafia enforcer who happened to work for the city government. That being said, he never raised a hand against me or my sister. He was strict and he was cold, but he never hit us. He never raised his voice when he disciplined us, either, but simply rebuked us in a cold, scornful voice, his eyes like chips of ice, the knuckles standing out against his skin as he flexed his fingers.

When I got older I realized that he was a very damaged man who was trying to be the best father he could with what was left of his conscience.

Dad was also a bit paranoid, for excellent reasons that I found out later. He had a gun concealed in every room of our house, and he taught me and Maggie how to shoot and the basics of self-defense. Our house was a fortress, with bars over the windows and reinforced steel security doors. I had one room on the second floor, Maggie had the second, and we never, ever went into my dad's room for any reason ever. Sometimes when he opened and closed the door, I saw the rifles mounted on the wall, along with things he had brought back from his time in Afghanistan.

The Kane household was a well-armed one, and Dad made sure things ran like clockwork. Despite that, he really didn't care what we did with our designated leisure time, which is why Maggie and I were playing a video game when the hour of Invasion Day came.

I remember it so clearly. It was about nine at night on a Saturday. Dad was in the gym, which is what he called the dining room since we didn't have a table and it was full of exercise equipment, grunting to himself as he lifted weights. Maggie and I had finished our chores, so we sat in front of the TV, game controllers in hand as we played a racing game.

"Roland, the console is overheating again," said Maggie. She was thirteen years old, and because of Dad's training she was a bit of a tomboy, so we got along pretty well. Her thumbs jabbed at the controller, her face narrowed in concentration as she focused on the game. She had Dad's focus and intensity, but she looked a lot like Mom. I don't think she remembered Mom very well. I suspect Maggie had been my parents' last attempt at making peace before she left.

"I don't think it is," I said. "The game's still working." Our model of game console had this bad habit of overheating and frying itself, rendering itself incapable of doing anything but putting a big red ring on the screen. We'd already replaced the stupid thing twice under the warranty. "I don't hear the fan going. If it was about to overheat again, the fan would be on maximum."

Maggie scowled as she steered her car around one of the track's hazards. "You don't hear that?"

"Hear what?" I said.

"That whining noise. It sounds like the fan is maxing out again."

"It really doesn't," I said. I was mostly concentrating on the game, but come to think of it I did hear a faint whining noise. It didn't sound like a computer fan. It sounded higher than that. Almost like metal tearing.

I paused the game.

"Hey!" said Maggie. "You're just doing that because I was winning."

"Hang on," I said. I scooted closer to the TV, listened to the game console for a moment, but I didn't hear anything from the box. I heard the fans, yes, but they sounded normal. I heard Dad grunting as he did deadlifts, the floor vibrating a little every time he dropped the barbell.

And I heard that strange metallic whine. It seemed to be getting louder. Maybe there was something wrong with the air conditioner?

"Roland."

Dad had come into the living room. He was a big man, and he looked like the sort of cop who would kick down doors and come in with his carbine blazing. He kept his head shaved, even though it kind of made him look like a Nazi, but I think the comparison pleased him. Right now, he had a massive scowl on his face, and I cringed a little. If that whining sound ticked him off and he thought it was coming from the game console...

"Yeah, Dad?" I said.

"Mute that," he said. "I need to listen."

I nodded and hit the mute button on the remote. The game's chipper music went quiet, and I could hear that whining sound. It was now louder than the noise coming from the console's fans.

"It must be the air conditioner," pronounced Maggie. She tended to be a bit of a know-it-all. "That sounds like an air conditioner motor."

"Maybe one of the neighbors is fixing something," I said. "Or their car won't start."

"No, it must be the air conditioning," said Maggie. "A broken car doesn't make that noise."

I looked up at Dad to see what he thought, and I blinked in surprise.

There was something on his face that I had never seen before.

Dad looked…

He was frightened.

"Dad?" I said.

He didn't say anything. I don't think I can describe how shocking this was. Dad never showed fear about anything, ever. Chicago at that time wasn't exactly a safe place, and people had tried to break into our house a couple of times. Dad had beaten the would-be burglars within an inch of their lives, his scowl never wavering. For him to show fear was as shocking as if the sun had gone dark in the middle of the day or had risen in the west.

"Dad?" said Maggie, concern in her voice.

"Oh, no," he said in a quiet voice. "No, no, no. Not now. Not now." He looked at Maggie and me. "I had really hoped you two would be spared this."

"What's wrong?" said Maggie.

Dad seemed to pull himself together, his face drawing into its usual hard mask. "Get your grab bags and go. We leave in five minutes."

I pushed to my feet, puzzled, but I knew better than to disobey. "What's going on?"

"And get your guns," said Dad. I blinked at that. As you might guess, Dad was a gun nut, but he was equally fanatical about gun safety, and he had drilled into us that we were never to pick up a gun in a crisis unless we needed to use it, and never to point the weapon at anything unless we intended to kill it. "Guns, grab bags, kitchen in the five minutes. Go!"

He all but shouted the last word, which kicked us into motion. Dad didn't shout. We scrambled up the stairs, and Maggie vanished into her bedroom, and I went into mine. My grab bag was in the closet. Dad was ever careful, and the grab bag had been loaded with clothes, food, tools, weapons, supplies—everything you needed to survive in a disaster or a crisis. Part of our chores included packing and repacking the grab bags, making sure that everything worked and that nothing had expired.

I pried up one of the floorboards in my room and took my gun from its hiding place.

I say "my" gun, but it was technically Dad's, and I was forbidden from touching it save at his express word or during a life-threatening emergency. It was a Glock 17 pistol, and while I would never win any shooting competitions, I was a decent shot with the thing. I checked that it was unloaded, and then pulled out the clips from the hiding place and tucked them into my grab bag.

Handling the heavy handgun seemed to send a shock through my brain. Before, the pure habit of obedience had taken over, but now I was beginning to wonder. Why were we doing this? All we had heard was an odd whining noise. Maybe it really was just the air conditioner acting up. The central air unit for our house was older than I was.

Then again, I had never seen Dad that freaked out by something. Angry, yes. He got angry and cold a lot. But frightened?

I shrugged, checked the grab bag one last time, and headed for the stairs. Maybe Dad was freaking out over nothing. If so, it was no big deal. Better to go along with what he had in mind than risk a punishment.

Maggie had beaten me downstairs, but she was always better organized than I was. Her eyes were wide in her face, though she seemed otherwise calm. I guess Dad's alarm must have gotten to her. The whining noise had gotten louder, so loud that it was starting to get annoying.

"I guess," said Maggie, "that's not really the air conditioner."

"No," I said. I started to point out that I had told her so, but I stopped. The noise had gotten louder, and it also sounded... strange. I had thought it sounded like a broken machine, but now it didn't sound like anything I had ever heard before, and it made the hair stand up on the back of my neck.

"It sounds like something screaming," said Maggie.

"Yeah," I said.

Then I saw the light.

It was nine o'clock at night, and the lights were off in the kitchen, the kitchen door closed. But around the edges of the door I saw a flickering, colorless light, almost like the fluorescent lights in a hospital emergency room. The light kept flickering, and I realized that it was flickering in time to the undulations of the whining noise.

"Roland," said Maggie. "I think that's coming from the alley."

I started to answer, and Dad came hurrying down the stairs. He was dressed in something that looked like riot gear—body armor and cargo pants and a harness for weapons. He was carrying a lot of weapons, two pistols, several grenades, a pair of heavy tactical knives, and he was holding an AR-15 with a lot of custom modifications.

"Dad," said Maggie. "If you go outside like that, you're going to get arrested."

"I'm not," said Dad. "The force is about to have bigger problems. In a couple of hours there might not even be a police force. Are you both ready?" We nodded. Dad looked at the glow coming from the kitchen and swore. "The alley. Of course it would have to be in the alley. Follow me. We're going to the SUV and getting out of here."

"What's going on?" I said, but we followed him.

He didn't answer as we walked into the kitchen. The lights were off, the blinds drawn, but the strange gray light leaked through the gap in the door and the windows. It flickered, the eerie whining sound altering in time to the light.

Dad froze for a moment at the back door, his hand an inch from the knob.

"Roland, Margaret," said Dad. "Listen to me. I hoped this would never happen. I've been preparing for this day for years, but I prayed you wouldn't have to live through this. Guess I'm not going to get what I want. Our lives are going to change, and they're going to change for the worse." He looked at us with hard eyes. "If we're going to get through this, you're going to have to do whatever I tell you, and we're going to have to stick together. You understand?"

"You're starting to scare me, Dad."

"Good. Tell me you understand."

"We understand," Maggie and I chorused.

"No," said Dad. "Say it."

"We… have to do what you say, and stick together," I said.

"What Roland said," said Maggie. "Do what you say, and stick together."

"All right," said Dad. He took a deep breath, and I suddenly realized he was steeling himself to face whatever was outside. It was the most frightening thing I'd ever seen in my life. "Let's go."

He threw open the door and strode into the backyard, and Maggie and I followed him.

And for the first time in my life, but definitely not the last, I saw one of the Dark gates.

Chapter 2
The Coming of the Dark

Yes, I know they're not "gates", not really. I've heard the official scientific description, filled with words like bosons and tachyons and anti-protons and wormholes and tunneling neutrino streams, and I've seen the equations the scientists worked out. I think all the math written out to describe one of the gates scientifically takes something like five hundred pages.

So the thing I saw hovering at the end of the alley behind the house wasn't really a gate, but that was sort of what it looked like.

It was like a… hole in the air, a rip made out of flickering gray light. The wailing, whining noise came from it, almost as if the air was screaming from having that hole ripped through it. Through the gate, I saw someplace else. It looked kind of like a jungle, albeit a jungle filled with giant mushrooms that glowed with a purplish-black light and vines that pulsed and throbbed like mobile veins. Through gaps in the mushrooms I saw a writhing red sky, black lightning leaping from twisted thunderhead to twisted thunderhead.

It looked like a kind of hell.

"Dad," said Maggie, shocked. "What is…"

"Don't talk," he said. "Don't stop. Keep walking. Right to the garage. Go."

We kept walking. Our yard wasn't wide, but it was deep. Dad had a little plastic shed for storing lawn equipment, though he had never more than a perfunctory interest in keeping the lawn trimmed. I glanced at the shed as we passed, perhaps because it seemed so normal compared to the weird thing in the alley.

As I looked, a dark shape moved from behind the shed, and for the first time, I saw one of the Darksiders.

At first I thought it was a big dog. Then it moved out from behind the shed, and I realized that it was moving wrong for a dog because it had too many legs. The thing came into the light shining from the gate, and I got a better look at it.

"Dad!" I shouted.

It was hideous, absolutely hideous. It had twelve jointed legs like those of a giant spider, but the twelve legs supported a curved shell kind of like that of a giant sea creature. Spines jutted almost at random from the shell, and its two forelimbs looked like those of a scorpion, with serrated cutting edges. Its head was a misshapen mass of black chitin and red eyes, seemingly jammed together at random, and it twitched back and forth as it scanned the backyard.

This thing was nothing close to human. It was nothing even close to something that belonged on this Earth.

"Daddy!" screamed Maggie, but Dad was already moving into action.

The armored thing surged forward, rearing up on its back legs as it did so. A mouth opened at the front of the creature, four interlocking jaws yawning wide, their edges marked with serrated blades.

Dad shot it five times. The creature shrieked and black slime erupted from the creature as all five shots struck its head. The creature staggered and collapsed, going silent.

"What was that?" I said. My voice sounded strange in my ears.

"Scout drone," said Dad. "I think I got it before it could contact the hive mind. Now go! We wait too long, there will be hundreds of those things swarming over the yard."

I had a million questions, but the habit of obedience was stronger than my curiosity and my fear, and I ran after Dad as he and Maggie jogged to the garage. It was a two-car garage, but half the space was taken up by Dad's workbenches and equipment lockers. Dad drove a big black SUV that looked the kind of vehicle that would be driven by spooks for Homeland Security or the FBI or something, and he yanked out his key and unlocked the back.

"Roland, Maggie," he snapped, pointing at some of the footlockers. "Get boxes one, two, four, and seven. I'm going to start the car." He jogged around and started the engine, and Maggie and I started hauling the labeled footlockers to the SUV, straining under the weight. It took both of us to move just one of them. Dad saw us straining, grimaced to himself, and rushed to help us. Together Maggie and I could move one of the lockers, but he picked up two at once and dumped them in the back of the SUV.

I caught my breath. Looking back, the lockers hadn't been all that heavy, not compared to some of the loads I've carried since, but I was only sixteen and I had that pack on my back.

"Move," barked Dad. "Roland, take shotgun. Maggie, in the back. If I tell either of you to duck, do it."

I nodded and climbed into the passenger seat, while Maggie scrambled into the back. Dad climbed into the SUV, slamming the door behind him. He had already started the engine, which is kind of a dangerous thing to do in a closed garage, but he hit the garage door opener. The big door rattled open, and before it was even all the way up, he hit the gas and slammed into the alley, tires squealing as he swung the SUV around.

For a moment, the strange tear in the air was right behind us, and I stared into the hellish, twisted world on the other side. I saw the warped jungle, and I saw shapes moving beyond: huge, hulking beasts the size of houses, covered in spines and tentacles and claws and thousands of eyes.

The sight of them filled me with the same fear and crawling revulsion as the smaller creature that Dad had killed. For a wild instant, I wondered if the end of the world had come, if the Gates of Hell had opened and all the devils were coming out, and then Dad slammed on the gas. The SUV rocketed down the alley at reckless speed, blurring past the neighbors' garages.

In the streetlight ahead I saw something skittering at the end of the alley.

A lot of somethings.

Nearly a half-dozen of those smaller creatures, the things that Dad had called drones, moved back and forth between the alley and the street. As the SUV roared towards them, all the creatures turned and started scuttling towards us.

"Dad," I said.

"Hang on!" he said, and he pushed the gas harder.

The SUV roared and shot forward, and we ran over the drones. They were small enough and the SUV was big enough that we crushed them under our tires instead of having them slam into the radiator grill or into the hood. I heard a crushing, crunching sound, and black slime spattered across my window. The SUV jerked and bucked, and for an awful instant I was sure that we had hit one of the creatures at exactly the right angle to send us rolling.

Then we screeched into the street and Dad spun the wheel in a right turn. I looked back and saw that we had crushed four of the creatures into pools of glistening black pulp, while the remaining two pursued us in vain.

And as I looked, I saw something bigger emerge from the gate in the alley.

Something maybe about the size of a human, but definitely not human. I had a brief glimpse of a thing that looked vaguely like a giant armored insect, and then the SUV tore down the street. For a moment, everything looked normal, and I almost found it hard to believe I had just seen a hole in the air disgorging giant insect-monsters. Rows of parked cars stood along the curbs, and here and there I spotted people smoking on their front steps or talking into their cell phones.

Then I saw a flicker of gray light behind one of the house, and as we drove past, I glimpsed another one of those gates, the black shapes of drones jumping through it. As I looked, I heard the distant wail of a police siren.

Then another, and another, and the distant rapid pop of gunshots.

"Dad," I said.

He didn't say anything, his mouth a hard line, his knuckles shining white against his skin as he gripped the wheel.

"Dad," I said again. "What's happening?"

"Don't you have to go to work?" said Maggie in a small voice. "I mean, you're a law enforcement officer," Dad had trained us never to use the word cop, "and if something bad is happening, don't you have to go to work?"

"No," said Dad. "Not this time. Family's more important, and the entire Chicago PD is going to be dead in the next day, along with most of Chicago."

"Those things in the alley," I said. "You know what they are."

"Yeah." He fell silent and I thought he wouldn't say anything more, but then he kept talking. "You know I was in the army before I joined the department."

I nodded.

"I learned some classified stuff in the army," said Dad. "I knew these things would come someday. That's why I've been getting ready. I didn't prep up and train you two just because I was afraid of riots or civil war or the government collapsing, though it never hurts to be prepared. No, I did all this because I knew they were coming someday. I had hoped…" His voice trailed off, and he shook his head. "I hoped it would come after your lifetimes. Guess I hoped wrong."

We were doing at least thirty over the speed limit, and had turned onto a street lined with strip malls and small shops. Dad passed a bus on the right, and I caught a glimpse of the driver glaring at us. So far everything seemed calm, but if all of those gates started disgorging creatures like the drones, or even bigger monsters, then a panic would spread quickly. And when the police fought back, they would call in the National Guard and the army or maybe even the Air Force or something.

Chicago was going to become a war zone.

No wonder Dad wanted to get out now.

"What are they?" I said.

I didn't think he was going to answer, but after a moment he did.

"Don't rightly know," he said. "I don't think anyone does. Army intel always just called them the Dark. Stupid name, scares everyone, but it stuck. They're probably aliens. They might be devils from Hell. They might even be from the past or the future or something. I don't know. But whenever they come out of those gates that open up, and they can open anywhere, they kill everyone they can catch."

"This has happened before?" said Maggie.

"Yeah, couple of times," said Dad, pushing the gas a little further. He ran a red light, and I flinched as we came within a few feet of hitting an oncoming truck. Dad swerved around it, the tires screeching, almost went onto the curb, and resumed driving. "Usually it happens out in Idaho or Nevada or someplace isolated like that, and the government covers it up. They take out any Darksiders that come through and shoot anyone who talks too much. But if the Dark is opening this many gates in a major urban area, they're coming for us in a big way. It's going to be a war like no one's ever seen before."

"Then where are we going?" said Maggie.

"Washington State," said Dad. "I know some people in the army. They've been getting ready for this, even if no one else has, the idiots." He shook his head. "We get out of Chicago fast enough, we ought to avoid the worst of it. Getting over the Mississippi will be tricky once the panic starts. The U.S. Highway 52 bridge is our best bet. Mostly rural, and..."

He swore and slammed on the brakes as a huge shape out of a nightmare lumbered onto the street ahead.

Just looking at the thing made my stomach twist. Something about it reminded me of an elephant, though it was much larger than any elephant. It stomped along on eight legs that looked like folding knives of black glass, their tips digging chunks from the asphalt. An armored shell that looked like an armadillo squatted atop those legs, a vast maze of tentacles lashing at the air from its front and back. Dozens of small black shapes circled around the huge creature, and some of them broke away, heading towards us.

Dad swore again, spun the wheel, and hit the gas, while the black shapes pursued us. As they drew closer, I saw that they looked kind of like deformed, glistening mantises, albeit mantises the size of baseball bats. The SUV roared as it hurtled forward, and we outpaced almost all of the flying things.

One slammed into the back window and landed there. There was a horrible squealing noise, its bladed forelimbs sliding against the window, and I realized that it was cutting through the glass.

"Maggie!" shouted Dad. "Shoot it!"

Maggie stared at the creature, her eyes huge in her face. Dad had trained us well, but we had never seen anything like that monster before. Shooting a human was one thing. It wasn't all that different than shooting targets at the range, as I would find out later. But Maggie had never seen the mantis-thing before, and the shock and horror of it made her freeze up.

"Down!" I said, twisting around in my seat. "Down, down!"

Maggie dropped to the seat, and I gripped my pistol with both hands and started shooting.

My first shot missed and punched a hole in the back window. My second shot caught the creature in its center of mass. I had no idea where the vital points were on the mantis-thing, but aiming for the center of mass was always a good idea. I squeezed the trigger again, and this time the creature jerked off the window and hit the road behind us, spewing black fluid as it rolled away. The sight made me briefly think of a full soda bottle thrown out of the back of a moving card.

"You okay?" I said.

Maggie nodded and straightened up, shivering.

"You're going to have to toughen up," said Dad, his eyes back on the road. "Those things are going to be everywhere. It's going to be a hard trip to Washington State. Understand?"

Maggie didn't say anything.

"Margaret," said Dad. "Do you understand?"

At last she nodded. "I do. I understand. I'm sorry. I just got frightened. I…"

"Don't apologize," said Dad. "Do better next time. If we're going to get to Washington alive, we need to watch out for each other."

We lapsed into silence as Dad drove as fast as he could, and around us, I heard more and more sirens and more of the strange whining noise from the gates.

We got out of Chicago alive. It took the better part of a day, but we got out alive.

I've since spoken with other survivors of Invasion Day in Chicago, and Dad's paranoia paid off. We got out before the first major wave of Darksiders came through the gates, and before the panic and riots started. There were riots, of course. A large portion of the city's population decided to take advantage of the chaos to descend on Michigan Avenue for some retail therapy via looting, only to be slaughtered when winged Darksiders fell on them. Central authority collapsed, and Chicago degenerated into chaos, with every man for himself.

Millions of people died. Or were taken.

More on that later.

We headed west on U.S. Highway 52. There wasn't a lot of traffic. From time to time we saw that people had started building barricades across the freeway, and Dad turned off and headed through the county roads. He seemed to have a surprising knowledge of the back ways of Illinois, and he put it to good use, avoiding the major towns along the highway. It almost seemed like a pleasant drive in the country.

Almost. Except for a few oddities.

Like the lack of traffic.

Or the fact that most of the radio stations had gone off air, and those that were on seemed to be either people begging for the military to help them or people ranting that the end of the world had come and Jesus had returned to judge mankind. Or the occasional barricades we saw piled up on roads or by houses, or the plumes of smoke we sometimes saw in the distance. Dad checked his cell phone from time to time, but there was no signal. He said that it meant the Dark had opened gates in the other major cities, that this was not just a raid but an invasion.

We were attacked twice.

The first time was when we stopped alongside a county road so Dad could get some rest before driving into the night. As soon as we stopped, three Darksiders of the kind that we had shot in the backyard attacked, heading straight for us. Fortunately, we were on our guard, and we had a clear field of fire. All three of us started shooting, and we took down the horrible creatures before they reached us. The last one came to a twitching stop about a yard from my feet.

"Don't touch it, Roland," said Dad. I jerked back from the creature. "The venom in its pincers can stay active for hours after it's dead."

"Yes, sir," I said.

We had to drive to a new place to camp, and spent a restless night watching for more Darksiders.

The second time we got into a gunfight, Dad shot two people.

We were on a county road in a wooded part of western Illinois. The road went around a curve, and Dad slowed down. As he did, we saw a van pulled across the road. There were two men in jeans and brown coats standing there, both of them holding shotguns.

"I was afraid of this," said Dad, bringing the SUV to a stop. "Wait here."

He slid out of the car and walked forward, hands spread to show that he wasn't carrying any weapons. The two men in tan jackets approached him, shotguns held low. I couldn't hear what they were saying, but Dad was smiling more than he usually did, and soon he had the men nodding along with him.

Then the men glanced into the trees, and Dad drew his Glock and shot them both.

It happened so fast that I barely saw it. The two men in tan jackets never saw it coming. One moment they were living, breathing men. The next they were dead on the asphalt, their blood and brains pooling beneath them. Dad grimaced for a moment, shook his head, and looked back at the SUV.

"Maggie, Roland, get out here," said Dad. "We'll need to take their weapons and any useful supplies they have."

I climbed out of the SUV, too shocked to argue, and Maggie followed suit. Dad opened the back of the dead men's van, flinched, and then closed the door.

"No," he said. "On second thought, we'll just go."

I could smell the blood in the air, mixed with the familiar odor of gun smoke.

"You killed them," I whispered.

"Yeah," said Dad, as if I was stating the obvious.

"But you just murdered them!" I said. "They didn't do anything to us, and you just shot them in the head so we can take their stuff."

Dad stared at me for a moment. He looked like he had been carved out of stone.

"Come with me," said Dad. "Both of you. You need to see something."

I hesitated, but as horrified and as angry as I was, obedience was a lifelong habit. Dad walked into the trees, and Maggie and I followed him. I noticed that a lot of the undergrowth had been trampled, and tire tracks marked the dirt. Dad stepped around a big oak tree, and I stopped in sudden shock, my gorge rising.

Two cars sat in a small clearing, and dumped on the ground were a dozen dead people, men, women, and children. All of them had been shot. Maggie let out a little shriek, one hand flying to her mouth.

"I saw the tracks from the road," said Dad. "Figured we'd run into something like that sooner or later. Those two rats on the road had set up a little ambush. They've been stopping people fleeing the city, killing them, and taking their stuff. In a few days, when the smell gets too bad, they'll go somewhere else and do it again." He gripped our shoulders, the hand against my shoulder still holding his Glock. "Listen to me. We're going to see a lot of things like this in the next few years. If we're going to survive, we're going to have to be hard, and we're going to have to trust each other. Understand?"

I nodded, too sickened to speak.

Dad hesitated, and then nodded back. "I'm sorry you had to see that."

Without another word, we walked back to the SUV, steered around the van, and kept going.

Chapter 3

The Drive

We got across the Mississippi without incident. After the ambush on the country road, I feared that bandits would have set up on the bridge, but I guess the two men Dad killed had been ahead of the curve. On the bridge was a long line of heavily loaded cars and trucks fleeing to the west, away from Chicago, and while the mood was tense and it took a long time to cross the bridge, there wasn't any violence. The fact that everyone I saw was openly carrying weapons helped keep a civil air.

Dad talked to a grim-faced old man in a pickup truck, a bandoleer of shotgun shells across his chest. He had come from Dubuque, and the town had been destroyed by the Dark after a dozen gates opened up in the heart of the city. Dad questioned him for a few moments, and then suggested that he head towards eastern Washington State, where Dad was confident that the military would be in control of the situation.

Which made me wonder where we were going and why.

"Where are we going?" I asked once we had gotten over the Mississippi. Dad had abandoned U.S. Highway 52, taking instead a maze of county roads through the cornfields of Iowa.

"Eastern Washington State," said Dad, his eyes on the road. Far to the west I saw a plume of smoke, but other than that there were no threats in sight.

"Yeah, but why?" I said. "I mean… those Darksider things are everywhere. Why would going to Washington be any safer than going anywhere else? We're not going to Seattle, are we?"

"No," said Dad with a contemptuous snort. "Seattle? The Mecca of hippies?" He sobered a little. "I suppose they're all dead, though. The Dark would have opened gates there as well."

"But why would we be any safer out there than we would be here?" I said, gesturing at the rows of corn passing us by. "Do you have like… I don't know, a bunker out there or something?"

"No," said Dad.

He didn't seem inclined to answer further, and I gave up.

Maggie leaned forward. "Dad… you knew in advance this was going to happen."

Dad didn't say anything.

"Why didn't you warn anyone?" said Maggie.

He let out a tired sigh. "No one would have believed me. If you had gone on the Internet, you could have found a billion sites claiming that aliens would invade Earth any day now." He grimaced. "That, and official government policy was to neutralize anyone who went around telling people the truth about the Dark. They feared a panic. Well, they've got their panic now, the idiots. Why didn't they listen?"

"Dad," said Maggie. "You said we have to trust each other. If you didn't trust the government… maybe it is time to trust us instead."

He glanced at her for just a moment. He never treated us differently, but I suspected that he liked her better than he liked me. No, that wasn't quite right. I think he loved us both in his own harsh way, but Maggie was just more persuasive than I was.

"You know I was in the army," he said at last. "Afghanistan. While we were there, the Dark opened a gate near Kandahar, and my company had to fight them off. We drove them back and closed their gate—they use this crystal thing the scientists call a transductor to open the gates, and the only way to permanently close a gate is to go through it, grab the transductor, and retreat back to Earth with the crystal." He scratched his jaw for a moment, the stubble rasping under his fingernails. "After that, the Division talked to us."

"The Division?" I said.

"Covert force in the U.S. Army in charge of dealing with the Dark," said Dad. "General Culver is their commanding officer. Bill Culver." He scowled. "He was sharp, but of course, the morons in the Pentagon didn't listen to him. They never listened to him. Maybe if they had, a lot of people might still be alive. Anyway, I left the Army and joined the Chicago PD, but those of us who were in the Division had our orders. If the Dark showed up in force, we were all to go to Castle Base in eastern Washington. That's where the Division is based, and General Culver will be basing a resistance force there."

"If he's still alive," I said.

"He'll be alive," said Dad with complete confidence. "Bill Culver and the men at Castle Base know more about the Dark than anyone else. They've been planning for this day for years. Maybe decades." He sighed.

"It's bad, isn't it?" I said.

"Very," said Dad. "I knew this was bound to happen someday. Didn't know when. Hoped it wouldn't happen in my lifetime, but you two are so young, I figured it might well happen in yours." He sighed again and rubbed his jaw. "That's why I've been so hard on you. I knew this could happen. So I tried to get you ready, so you can stay alive."

"What will we do when we get to Castle Base?" I said.

"I don't rightly know," said Dad. "General Culver will be putting together a force to fight the Dark, so I guess I'm rejoining the U.S. Army. Assuming there is still a U.S. government, of course. You kids… I'll make sure you're taken care of. I don't know what you'll do, exactly. Maybe the Division will have a school or something, but you'll likely be given jobs to earn your keep. We've never done this kind of thing before, so we'll play it by ear."

We made it all the way to Wyoming before everything fell apart.

I'm not sure exactly where it happened. We were somewhere in eastern Wyoming, in the more arid regions. There were a lot of rocky hills and a lot of scrub grass and the air felt dry and harsh and hot. It was about ten in the morning, and we had pulled over to relieve ourselves. It wasn't safe to wander off alone for obvious reasons, which made for some awkwardness. I didn't mind Dad and Maggie watching while I relieved myself (I could turn my back, after all), but Maggie absolutely hated doing her business when anyone could see her. I suppose girls have different needs in that department. So Dad had found her a nice boulder, and Maggie scuttled off behind it to heed nature's call while Dad I stood guard, guns in hand. We didn't talk. Dad discouraged casual chit-chat, unless I had questions of a practical nature, which I didn't at the moment.

I looked over the surrounding land, eyes squinting against the morning sunlight. The road was deserted, and I didn't see anything moving in the grass. I suppose the Dark could have been creeping along in the grass, or bandits might have been hiding behind the boulders, but I didn't see any sign of trouble.

Dad waited with an air of patience that I found difficult to emulate. I felt exposed standing out here, but I supposed Dad knew better than to rush a girl in the bathroom. I yawned, not bothering to cover my mouth (I needed both hands to shoot if necessary), turned around.

There were black specks in the sky to the west.

"Dad," I said.

He stepped next to me, gravel crunching beneath his boots. "I see them. Maggie, better hurry up. We might have to leave."

My first thought was that the black specks were vultures or buzzards. Ever since we had gotten over the Mississippi we had seen carrion birds circling over a lot of car wrecks and burning towns. The Dark might be wiping out humanity, but the vultures and the crows were doing well out of it. Except that vultures and buzzards tended to circle a lot, and crows traveled in big groups. I only saw a dozen of the specs, and they were flying perfectly level. Helicopters? For a wild instant, I hoped that the army had sent helicopters to rescue us, that maybe Dad's friend General Culver had sent men out to find him.

But the black specks were too small to be helicopters, and they were flying too fast. And too quiet.

They were also headed right for us.

"Dad," I said. "Flying things!"

"Maggie, hurry up!" shouted Dad. "We're about to be under attack!"

Maggie scrambled up from behind her boulder, doing up the front of her jeans with one hand, her other grasping the handle of her pistol. She started to run for the SUV, but Dad stopped her with an upraised hand.

"No," he said. "They're too fast. They'll rip the roof off the SUV. Now they've seen us, they won't let us go."

"Darksiders?" I said.

Dad nodded. "Different type of scout drone. Flyers. They'll try to kill us or disable us, and then go find some warriors to convert us." At the time, I didn't know what that meant, but it did sound dangerous. "We're going to have to fight. We can't let a single one of them get away. Even one of them gets away, they'll summon reinforcements and we're finished. Ready?"

I managed a sharp, jerky nod. Maggie offered a shaky nod as well, though her hands didn't shake as she held her gun.

"Say it," said Dad, still watching the approaching Darksiders.

"I'm ready," I said.

"Ready," said Maggie.

Dad nodded and raised his pistol, and we followed suit. By then, I could make out details of the approaching creatures. They looked a lot like the Darksider scout Dad shot dead in the backyard, but these creatures were bigger. Part of the extra mass was a massive bag of pulsating gray flesh that rose from the dorsal ridge of their shells, black veins threading through the quivering mass. I realized that those bags were kind of like the bags of a zeppelin or a balloon, full of hot gas that kept the creature aloft. The flying Darksiders also had blurring gossamer wings like those of a dragonfly, but far larger, and they looked somehow greasy.

"Aim for the bags!" shouted Dad, and he started shooting.

Maggie and I followed suit. There hadn't been time to put in any ear protection, and the crack of gunshots was loud in my ears. The noise the bullets made when they ripped through the Darksiders' gas bags was far louder. The bag exploded in a spray of fire and greasy flesh, causing the flyer to shriek and spiral to the ground.

That killed some of them. They hit the road or the desert with enough force to crack their shells, black slime spilling out. But some of them were able to survive the impact, and they rushed towards us, pincers and claws snapping.

"Take the flying ones!" Dad shouted, shifting his aim down. "I'll take the ones on the ground! Keep shooting, keep shooting!"

My gun clicked empty, and all the practice clicked in as I ejected the spent magazine and rammed another one into the weapon. With it reloaded, I shifted aim and sent more bullets into the sky. In a weird way, it was kind of like being at the shooting range, though the targets were much uglier.

We shot down the Darksiders in a storm of bullets. One by one they crashed against the ground, going motionless, or charged towards us and Dad shot them down. Maggie ejected a spent magazine from her gun and shoved another one into the weapon, and I covered her while she reloaded. Dad shot one of the grounded flyers, then another, and then another. The last creature raced towards him as my gun clicked empty, and Dad fired his final three bullets into it.

He killed it, but not before the Darksider slammed into him and drove him to the ground, its lethal pincers driving into his chest.

Dad landed with a startled grunt, and Maggie screamed and emptied her pistol into the side of the Darksider, the bullets punching through its armored black shell. The kinetic energy of the impacts knocked the creature to the side, and it rolled off Dad, dead, but one of its pincers had broken off in his chest, his shirt wet with blood.

"Dad!" said Maggie. "Daddy!"

She sprinted to his side. On pure reflex, I looked around, but the rest of the Darksiders were dead too. I ran to join Maggie as she fell to her knees next to Dad. I didn't know much about combat wounds, but I had a cold certainty in my chest that the injury was mortal. There was just so much blood. It was spreading out beneath him in a pool. His face had taken a grayish pallor, and his mouth opened and closed without sound.

"Dad," I said.

He reached into his jacket, yanked something out, and thrust it in my direction. It was a bundle of colorful papers. I took the papers, blinking away tears, trying to figure out what to do, and then he died.

He just died. There wasn't time to say anything, or to do anything. If this had been a movie or something, he would have told me to take care of my sister, and Maggie would have grabbed his hand as she sobbed, and he would have told us he loved us. Then he would have sighed, closed his eyes, and passed away.

Instead, he just sort of... stopped. Later on, I understood that he had died of a combination of massive blood loss and cardiac failure. The broken pincer had gone right through his heart, and it had been nothing short of astonishing that he had held on long enough to press those papers into my hand.

I stared at him, too stunned to react. Maggie was sobbing uncontrollably, grabbing his hand. I'm not sure what I felt at that moment, just... shock. Dad was invincible. He wasn't afraid of anything. Nothing in the world could possibly hurt him.

That jolted me a little into something like lucidity. Nothing in the world could hurt Dad, but the Dark hadn't come from this world. We might have wiped out that band of flying scouts, but others would be along eventually.

Those papers. Why had he given them to me? I opened the bundle. One was a road map of Washington State, with a location circled in red ink on the eastern side of the state, below the Cascade Mountains. Another was the business card of General William Culver, United States Army, and the third was an ID card in a leather holder. It was a picture of Dad, though much younger. He still had all his hair, though it was a buzz cut, and the card identified him as a member of the United States Army Rangers.

Castle Base. He had said that General Culver and the Division operated out of Castle Base. Did that mean Dad wanted us to continue to Castle Base? I looked at the SUV. We were in eastern Wyoming, and we needed to get to eastern Washington. How was I supposed to do that? I sort of knew how to drive, but it was nearly a thousand miles.

I looked at Dad's corpse again, and sort of lost it for a few minutes. I had been only sixteen, and while my upbringing hadn't been anywhere near normal or healthy, I was still only sixteen, and my entire life had been dominated by Daniel Kane's commanding presence. For him to die so suddenly was like the sun going out at midday. The destruction of Chicago and the invasion of the Dark had a strange, dreamlike feel to it.

My father's death seemed far more horribly, brutally real.

"Maggie," I said, once I pulled myself together. "Maggie, we need to go."

She looked up at my, bleary-eyed, tears running down her face.

"We can't stay here," I said, holding out the map towards her. "This is the way to Castle Base. I think Dad wanted us to go there. If we stay here, the Darksiders will kill us too."

"We can't just leave Dad here," protested Maggie.

I started to say that we couldn't take him with us. A cold, practical voice in my mind that sounded exactly like Dad's pointed out that driving across the country with a corpse in the back seat would likely lead to disease, to say nothing of the smell.

"Dad's not here anymore." I pointed to his body. "That's not him, Maggie. You know what he would tell us to do."

"Yeah," said Maggie. She took a deep breath, her whole body shaking with it, and then forcibly calmed herself down. Her face became a mask of pure emotional control. "He'd tell us to keep moving, not to look back."

There may have been a lot of Daniel Kane's remorseless practicality in me, but there was at least some of it in his daughter too.

"All right," I said. "We don't look back. We move on."

"Do you even know how to drive?" said Maggie.

"Sort of," I said. Dad had been showing me. "I'll go slow. You watch for the Dark and bandits."

Chapter 4

Castle Base

I had to kill my first man two days later.

We made a stupid mistake. We stopped at a rest area in Idaho to use the toilets. In my defense, after several days of relieving myself in the woods and trying to clean myself up with leaves, using an actual working toilet seemed like a vision of heaven. So, I pulled over to the rest stop (without going over the curb this time), a squat cinder block building, and Maggie and I went to use the bathrooms.

She started screaming as soon as she went into the women's room.

I ran to the women's room door just as a burly man dragged Maggie out, her arms pinned behind her back. He had a big gut, but his arms were just as thick, and he was smiling as if he had just found a twenty dollar bill in the gutter. His left arm held Maggie's arms pinned, but his right hand held a shotgun pointing towards the ground.

I didn't hesitate. I raised my pistol, aimed, and shot him through the temple.

That made a mess, but Maggie jerked free as he collapsed, and she yanked her own gun from its holster.

"He was hiding behind the door in the women's room," she said, breathing hard, her pistol pointed at the motionless man. "I think he was waiting for us…"

"Yeah," I said. "Let's look around and make sure there aren't any more of them about to ambush us."

As it turned out, he had been operating alone. We found his van parked behind the building. Inside his van he had a lot of ammunition, and he also had sets of handcuffs, rubber gloves, and a lot of drugs and syringes.

I was pretty sure I knew why he had tried to kidnap Maggie.

Maggie knew, too. She was noisily sick next to the van. I waited until she finished, then together we helped ourselves to the dead man's foodstuffs, ammunition, and shotgun, and loaded them into the SUV. As we did, I glanced at the corpse by the restroom, and was surprised that I didn't feel anything. I mean, you're supposed to be consumed with guilt and sorrow when you kill your first man, right?

I didn't feel any of that. Mostly I felt satisfaction. He deserved it. I was pretty sure Maggie had not been his first attempt at kidnapping.

Yeah, I had a lot of my father in me.

We drove on.

Our luck ran out a little west of Spokane.

By mutual agreement, Maggie and I gave Spokane a wide berth, keeping to the side roads. From miles away, we had seen the plumes of smoke rising from Spokane, and I guessed that the Dark had opened a bunch of their gates inside the city. I suspected the wreckage of the city would be crawling with Darksiders, and I didn't want to bring Maggie anywhere near them, or any desperate survivors crawling out of the rubble.

"Roland," said Maggie, her voice tight.

I glanced at her. We were driving down a narrow county road, pine trees rising on either side of us. Based on the map that Dad had given me in his final moments, I thought we were about a hundred and fifty miles from Castle Base, maybe two hundred if we had to go further out of our way.

I looked at her, and then back at the road, and saw the man waiting for us.

He was a cop, a Washington State trooper, to judge from his uniform. He was standing right in the middle of the road, and I slowed down. I had a flood of hope. Maybe law and order was still functioning in this part of the country, and I could find an adult to take charge and get me and Maggie to safety.

Then I saw his eyes.

They were black. Like, I don't mean the irises were black. The pupils, irises and the whites had all turned the same black as the armored shells of the Darksider drones. The trooper began walking towards us, and I saw that black veins bulged beneath his skin, and his skin itself had turned a pallid, corpse-like gray.

He looked like a zombie. But he wasn't dead, not completely. The fist-sized lump of black flesh pulsing at the base of his neck saw to that. It was a Darksider parasite, and it had sunk its tendrils into the trooper's spinal column and rewritten his nervous system and his DNA. It wiped the trooper's mind and turned him into a drone under the control of the Dark's hive mind. The scientists had some long Latin word to describe the process, but since zombie TV shows were popular right before Invasion Day, we just called those who had been taken zombies.

Unlike most of the zombies on TV, the converted people were just as fast and as strong as they had been in life. In fact, they were stronger, since they were immune to pain and unconcerned about injury.

Unfortunately, I didn't know any of this at the time.

"What do you think is wrong with him?" I said.

The trooper was striding towards us, unblinking black eyes fixed upon the SUV.

"He looks sick, I think," said Maggie, shifting her grip on her pistol. "Do you think we should stop and help him?"

"No," I said. "If he's sick, he might transmit it to us. And look at him. That black stuff in his eyes looks like something from the Dark."

"Then get us out of here," said Maggie.

I still really didn't know how to drive properly, but after several days of handling the SUV by myself, I was at least more competent. I pushed on the gas, and the big vehicle surged forward. The trooper ran towards us, and I steered around him. He threw himself at the SUV, and his hands scraped against Maggie's window, but he wasn't able to find any purchase on the smooth glass and soon I saw him in the rearview mirror. He ran after us, then he turned, stopped, and resumed his position.

"He's just waiting there," said Maggie, looking back over the seat.

"Yeah," I said, looking at the stubby pine forest on either side of us. This part of Washington State was pretty dry, and the pine trees looked a bit stunted, but there was plenty of cover for either Darksiders or zombies to be hiding on either side of the road. "He must be a lookout. Which means…"

Movement erupted from the trees in front of us, and nearly a dozen zombies in State Trooper uniforms sprinted onto the road, moving to block us.

The zombie on the road had been a lookout.

My sister screamed. My initial impulse was to hit the brakes to keep from hitting anything, but my foot missed and hit the gas instead. The SUV roared forward, and we slammed into the zombies. I heard an awful crunching noise as the fender smashed into two of them, followed by a jolt as we ran them over. Another zombie jumped onto the hood, but rolled away.

A fourth one threw itself forward just as we passed, and it smashed through the driver's side window, its hands coiling around my throat. The fingers felt hot, so hot that it was almost painful, but that was barely noticeable next to the pain as the hands cut off my breath.

I would have screamed, but I couldn't draw breath to do it. The SUV swerved as I fought to get the zombie off me, and I desperately tried to steer with one hand while shoving at the zombie with the other. The thing heaved itself forward, so close that I could have kissed its face. It had once been a state trooper, and I saw the black veins threading beneath the gray skin of its face, saw the eyes filled with blackness, and a strange sickly sweet smell came off the creature.

The creature opened its mouth and vomited on me.

Absurd as it was, my first thought was annoyance that the thing had sprayed black slime all over my face and chest. I didn't have that many clean clothes, and there was no way I could get that Darksider goop out of my shirt.

Then the pain exploded through my head, because the black slime it had sprayed on me was moving of its own volition. It surged into my nostrils and mouth. Panicked, I tried to clamp my jaw shut, but it was too late. The zombie was strangling me, and in my desperate attempts to draw a breath, I sucked the black slime down my throat and into my chest. It felt cold, horribly, horribly cold, yet I suddenly felt feverish.

I was clawing at the zombie's hands, so the SUV was swerving over the road back and forth as our struggles bumped against the steering wheel. My vision darkened, and then a roar filled my ears and the zombie's forehead exploded in a burst of brains and black slime. The iron fingers around my neck loosened, and the former state trooper fell from the side of the car, hit the road, and bounced away.

"Roland!" screamed Maggie. I couldn't tell if she was shouting a warning, expressing dismay, or telling me to drive better. Since the SUV was about to veer off the road and into the trees, I was pretty sure she was telling me to drive better. I got both hands around the wheel and swerved, getting the SUV more or less into the center of the road.

"What happened?" said Maggie. "Did it bite you? Are you hurt?"

"It... it didn't bite me," I said. My tongue felt thick and heavy, and I could still feel the remnants of that black slime sliding down my gullet. Mercifully, the stuff had neither taste nor smell.

It was just very, very cold, which was strange because I felt myself becoming feverish.

"That black slime," said Maggie, wiping at my face with her fingers.

"No!" I said. "Don't touch me! It might be poisonous..."

"It's gone," said Maggie, dread filling her voice.

Gone? I looked up at the rearview mirror and flinched. The slime was gone, but I could still see it spreading in black veins beneath the skin of my face.

Just like the state troopers who had attacked us.

"Roland," whispered Maggie. "Are you... are you going to turn into one of those things?"

"I don't know," I said. I should have been frightened. Mostly, I felt numb. I realized I was going to die. Dad had died, I was going to die next, and that would leave Maggie alone in a collapsing world full of the Dark and awful men like that pervert at the rest stop in Idaho.

That cut through the numbness. I couldn't let that happen. I had to make sure that Maggie was safe. That meant getting her to Castle Base before I succumbed to the poison the zombie had pumped into me.

Or before I became one of those creatures.

With cold clarity I realized that I might have to kill myself. For an instant I thought about asking Maggie to do it, but I rejected the idea. I couldn't do that to her. She would have to live with that memory for the rest of her life. I would have to do the hard thing, the cold thing, and make sure that she was safe from both the Dark and from me.

Just like Dad would have done.

Fortunately, there was a solution to both problems. Based on Dad's map, I thought we were only another sixty or seventy miles from Castle Base. I just had to get there. Then the Army could take care of Maggie, and if I was going to turn into a monster, they could shoot me.

"What are we going to do?" whispered Maggie.

"Castle Base," I said. "We have to get to Castle Base. They… they will know what to do. It's not much farther."

I managed another five miles before I began to have trouble driving. The muscle cramps were starting in my legs, and I was so feverish that sweat was pouring off me in rivers. Despite that, I was shivering so violently that I almost took the SUV off the road a few times. Maggie and I had to trade places. She took the steering, but she was just a little too short to reach the pedals, so I sat next to her and operated the gas and the brake with my left foot while she steered.

It was just as well that she was able to steer, because my fever got worse and worse, and as it did, I started to hear voices.

At first it was only a whisper, sibilant and insistent. Then it became a harsh rasp, stern and full of command. And then it became a mighty chorus, a hundred billion terrible voices joined in titanic unison, and I felt the overwhelming urge to obey that colossal voice, or maybe to fall down on my face and worship it. The great voice wanted me to kill, to kill and to kill until my heart burst within my chest.

It didn't matter. The part of my brain that remained rational pointed out that I was feverish enough to start hallucinating random crap.

I didn't do anything that the voices said. There was no way I was going to do anything else until I got Maggie to Castle Base. Then I could shoot myself in the head. Or, since my hands were shaking so badly, I could get one of the soldiers to do it for me. Dad had expounded with disgust, more than once, on idiots who tried to kill themselves with shotguns or drain cleaner and only wound up maiming themselves for life.

I was feverish enough that I found this funny, and I kept giggling. It says something about my state of mind that I was looking forward to getting shot in the head because then at least the stupid voices would shut up.

I don't remember the rest of the day clearly, only fragments.

First fragment: a large metal sign that said CASTLE BASE U.S. ARMY ACCESS RESTRICTED, and a chain link fence topped with barbed wire in the distance. Dry hills rose around us, dotted with scrub and ugly little trees.

The next thing I remember is lying on the pavement, the sky gray and overcast, the air dry against my face. Four men in camouflage stood over me, Army-issue M4 carbines in hand. Next to the soldiers stood a thirtyish man with a major's golden oak leaf on his uniform, and his nameplate read RANDOLPH.

I heard Maggie talking.

"My father sent us to find you," she said, the words tumbling out of her in a hurry. "We're supposed to see General William Culver at Castle Base. Daniel Kane, my father was named Daniel Kane."

"Sir, he's been contaminated," said one of the soldiers, his M4 pointing in my direction.

"I can see that," said Major Randolph. He squatted down to look at me, eyes narrowed. "What's your name?"

"Roland Kane," I said.

"He's stage three," said another of the soldiers.

"Let me guess," said Randolph, ignoring the soldier. "Someone with black eyes attacked you and spewed black slime into you, and then you got sick."

"Yes," I croaked.

"How long ago did that happen?" said Randolph.

"I... I don't remember," I said.

"About nine, ten hours," said Maggie. "Are you going to help him? He needs help."

"Nine hours?" said the first soldier. The man sounded incredulous. "That means he's been in stage three for at least seven hours. Maybe longer."

"Roland," said Major Randolph. "Do you hear voices inside your head?"

I managed to nod.

"What direction are they coming from?" said Randolph.

I noticed something that I had not earlier. Randolph had the usual insignia for a major in the United States Army, but there was something else. He had a little microphone pin on his collar. I don't mean an actual, working microphone, but a little bronze badge of an old-fashioned snowball microphone.

"The direction?" said Randolph.

"That way," I said, waving my hand towards his left.

Randolph and the soldiers all shared a look as if I had said something significant.

"He's just a kid, sir," said one of the soldiers.

"Get the general," said Randolph. "This is his call."

"Are you going to help my brother?" said Maggie. She sounded on the verge of tears of frustration.

"Yes," said Randolph. "If we can."

I blacked out for a while.

When I woke up I was in a hospital bed in what looked like an emergency room. My clothes were gone and I was wearing a hospital gown. There were a bunch of tubes and wires hooked up to my right arm, and I heard something beeping behind me. That should have alarmed me, but I was too tired to care.

A man in medical scrubs stood over me, frowning.

"He's awake, sir," said the medic, "but you'll have to be quick."

A paunchy, bald man with four gold stars on the shoulder of his camouflage uniform stepped to my side.

The way Dad had described General William Culver, I had expected him to look like the star of an action movie. In person, Culver looked like a slightly disheveled insurance agent, but a few details didn't ring true. No insurance agent had eyes that cold and hard and clear. When he spoke, even in a quiet voice, everyone in the room paid attention.

And the first time I saw him in Castle Base's gym, he could deadlift an astonishing amount of weight, so much that the bar was starting to flop like a noodle. He might have been able to break a man's neck with his bare hands without even needing to strain.

"Can you hear me, son?" said General Culver.

I managed to nod.

"Good," said Culver. "My name is General William Culver, commanding officer of Castle Base and the Black Division."

"My… my sister," I croaked. "Is she…"

"Safe," said Culver. "Some of the soldiers' wives are looking after her. I give you my word that whatever happens next, we will look after her and keep her safe here."

"Thank you," I said. I thought about what he had said. "What happens next?"

"You have to make a decision," said Culver. "And you have to make it right now, I'm afraid, because you're out of time. Did your father explain what happened to you?"

"No," I said. "He was killed before… I think it was Wyoming. We got hit by some flying Darksiders."

"I'm sorry for your loss," said Culver. "Daniel Kane was one of the most effective soldiers who ever served under my command." He stepped closer to the bed. "The Dark, as you may have guessed, use organic-based technology, and are part of a hive mind. The particular weapon that was used on you was designed to overwrite the DNA of your nervous system, converting you to a drone connected to that hive mind."

"The zombie," I said. "The zombie threw up some black slime into my face. Was that the weapon?"

"Technically, they're called the 'converted', but we usually just call them zombies too," said Culver. "Yes, that was the weapon. The length of the conversion process varies from victim to victim, but the ability to resist seems to depend on the native willpower of the victim. I shouldn't be surprised that Daniel Kane's son has lasted this long. But in the end, it will overcome you and you will become one of the converted."

"Guess you had better shoot me, then," I said, surprised at how calm I felt.

"That may not be necessary. There is a treatment for it," said Culver. "Normally, we would ask your father for permission to use it."

"But he's dead," I broke in.

"And there is no one else to ask," said Culver. "I doubt there is much left of the government at this point, but I would be within the scope of my authority to administer the treatment to you regardless of what you think. Still, you got your sister here alive and well, which is more than I would expect of a sixteen-year-old boy. So, I will put it to you plainly, and tell you the truth. The treatment may not work, and it might kill you. That being said, your death would be quick and painless, and it would certainly be preferable to living as one of the converted."

"Suppose I can't argue with that," I said. I didn't want to die. But I didn't want to turn into one of those things on the highway.

"If the treatment works, I will have to insist that you join Black Division," said Culver.

"Why?" I said, puzzlement overruling my fear. "I mean, it's like you said, sir. I'm just a kid. Yeah, my dad taught me to shoot and some other stuff, but I wouldn't be as useful as a real soldier."

"If the treatment succeeds," said Culver, "it will leave you with some unusual abilities that will be highly useful in our war against the Dark."

"Sir," said the medic, pointing at one of the displays alongside my bed.

Culver grimaced. "We're about out of time. Let me assure you that if the treatment works, you will acquire some abilities that will be of immense tactical and strategic utility against the Dark. To put it bluntly, we will need you. Your country will need you. Mankind itself, what is left of it, will need you." He spread his thick hands. "Those are your choices, Mr. Kane. If you prefer, we can euthanize you now. Or we can administer the treatment and give you a fighting chance. And if you survive, you will join us and help stop the Dark from doing worse than they've already done."

I didn't hesitate. I was too much my father's son to go down without a fight. And if it did work, well, the Dark had killed Dad and tried to kill Maggie. They had killed almost everyone I had ever known.

If there was going to be payback, then I wanted to be one of the ones dishing it out to them.

I looked the general in the eye and made myself speak as clearly as my aching throat could manage. "I understand the risks. I would like to take my chances with the treatment, sir."

"Good," said Culver, looking at the medic. "Do it."

The medic took a deep breath, nodded, and lifted an IV bag holding a purplish fluid. He crossed to my bedside and hooked it up to my IV line, and I watched as the purple stuff flowed down the clear plastic tube and into my blood.

"All right," said the medic. "This should induce uncon-sciousness in another minute or so. We'll know right away if it will work or not. And if not..."

He stepped aside, and for the first time I saw the two soldiers standing behind Culver, both of them holding M4s leveled at my chest.

"Good luck, son," said Culver.

"Thanks," I started to say, and then unconsciousness took me.

It wasn't sleep. It was something more profound.

And in that darkness, I dreamed.

I've never done drugs and have no desire to do so. Whenever I think about it, I hear Dad's voice lecturing me about the dangers of drugs, not because they were immoral or illegal or dangerous, but because they might impair my physical and mental capabilities in a moment of crisis. Before Invasion Day that had seemed like paranoia. After Invasion Day, it just seemed like good sense.

So I had never done drugs, but if I had, I might have been able to compare what I saw while unconscious to an LSD trip or perhaps a bad reaction to hallucinogens. A few of the other recruits who survived the process had more experience with recreational pharmacology, and they said it was just like smoking mushrooms.

Anyway, it wasn't a dream, and it wasn't an acid trip.

It was real.

In the vision, I could see time, and I could see how it was connected to gravity and space. If I had been lucid and had the proper mathematical knowledge, I could have sketched out the equations explaining it all. My mind expanded, and I saw the entire world floating in space, a sphere of blue and white in an infinite black void.

Black smears were spreading across the entire surface of the Earth.

The Dark. In my dream, I could see them, and I could feel them.

They were like a vast black cloud, moving from world to world, devouring their victims and moving ever onward. They could twist time and gravity together, letting them step from world to world like a man crossing a stream on stepping stones. I saw fingers of them reaching for Earth, sinking into it like poison into a bloodstream.

I watched the Dark start devouring our world, and as I watched, I gradually sensed that they were aware of me too.

In the dream, I didn't have sight or hearing or smell or any of the other senses, but I was aware of everything happening around me, and I was aware of the Dark. Their collective will and hive mind moved towards me, and I could feel them thundering inside of my head, their combined mind ancient and titanic and overwhelming.

A voice hammered into my mind, and it had one very simple message for me.

Submit. Images flashed through my thoughts, pictures of worlds they had destroyed, worlds with cities made of living glass, or worlds where the aliens living there had been able to manipulate gravity the way that humans could manipulate sound, worlds where the aliens had no idea what metal was, but could grow an entire city from a single seed. Submit. Submit.

The Dark devoured peoples. It devoured worlds. It devoured planets. It swept across the whole universe in a gargantuan black tide of blood and death.

That terrible tide, that irresistible force, turned its implacable will upon me and demanded that I submit.

I refused. They had killed my father and millions of other people. There was no way I would ever submit to them. To it. I snarled defiance at the black force, cursed it with every fiber of my being, totally indifferent to whatever it might to do me. And to my surprise, the vast will of the Dark recoiled before my angry resistance.

Then everything went black, and I found myself floating in peaceful nothingness. It was nice. If this was death, I decided I was okay with it.

Eventually I heard the beeping noise again. At first I thought a truck was backing up, but then I realized it was a heart monitor.

My gummy eyes blinked open.

I was still in the hospital bed in the emergency ward. Various wires and tubes were hooked up to me, and I heard people moving about the ward and talking in low voices. After a bit, I realized that I wasn't dead, and that I hadn't been shot.

That was good.

Come to think of it, I didn't feel all that bad. Absolutely exhausted, sure, but considering that I had been about to die from getting a face full of zombie goop, I didn't feel all that bad.

Except for one thing. My head felt strange. Not bad, not exactly, but very weird. I couldn't find the words to describe the sensations. I raised my hands to my face and head, worried that they had cut off my nose or something, but everything felt like it was where it should be.

"Roland?"

I blinked and turned my head.

Maggie was sitting in a chair next to my bed, and she leaned forward, her eyes wide with excitement.

"You're awake," she said.

"Yeah," I said.

"How do you feel?"

"Uh… good, I think," I said. "Little weird, but I'm all right."

She reached over, buried her face in my chest, and started to cry in relief. I put my arms around her and patted her on the back. I had to admit that I was tearing up a little myself. The air was dry in here, that was all.

"Are you okay?" I said, trying to make sense of the odd feeling in my head. My head didn't hurt. It didn't feel bad. It just felt strange, like I was hearing spikes of static, but all I could actually hear with my ears was Maggie and the hospital machines.

"Yeah," said Maggie, straightening up. She wiped at her eyes. "Better now, actually."

"Are they treating you well?" I said.

"They are," said Maggie again. "They're giving me things to do. Some computer work, some cleaning. Guns, mostly. They were surprised that I knew how to field-strip and clean an M4, but once they found out who Dad was, they said it made sense."

I started to think that there were child labor laws against that sort of thing, but civilization had collapsed, and they were feeding her. And it wasn't as if she could go back to school, get good grades, and go to college. Not that she would have gone to college, unless it was a teenage rebellion thing. Dad had very low opinions of college, and said we should learn how to do something useful.

"That's good," I said.

"I'm just glad you're awake," she said, wiping at her eyes. "None of the doctors were sure that you were going to wake up. General Culver visited a few times and said you were doing as well as could be expected, but I don't think any of them knew if you were going to wake up or not. Or if you would still be… you know…"

"Not a zombie," I said.

"Yeah," said Maggie.

I lifted my arms and said "braaaaaaains" in a low voice.

Maggie's eyes went wide, and then she burst out laughing and hit me on the shoulder.

"You hit me!" I said.

"You're not funny," she said, laughing.

"Then why are you laughing?" I said.

"Because you're not funny," said Maggie.

A boot clicked against the floor, and a man in fatigues walked up next to Maggie. He was somewhere in his middle thirties, lean with sharp lines cut into his face. He had a major's insignia on his uniform, and his name plate read RANDOLPH. After a moment, I recognized him. He was the major who had talked to us at the gate.

He still had that odd bronze microphone pin near his collar.

"Major Randolph," said Maggie.

"Mr. Kane," said Randolph. "My name is Major Philip Randolph, U.S. Army, Black Division. How are you feeling?"

"Better, sir," I said. "A little weird, though…"

"Let me guess," said Randolph. "It feels like you've got static inside your skull. If you turn your head right and left, the static seems to decrease or increase in strength, as if you were drawing closer or moving farther away from the sound. You can also feel several points of pressure in your skull. They're not painful, but it's like someone is tapping your skin. Am I right?"

I blinked in astonishment. That was exactly how I felt but had been unable to articulate.

"Yeah," I said. "Yeah, that's exactly it."

Major Randolph nodded. He looked pleased.

"Is that a side effect from the treatment?"

"Not quite," said Randolph. "Let's try something. The nearest source of pressure in your head. Point to where it feels like it is coming from."

I complied.

"The second nearest?" said Randolph.

I pointed in a different direction.

"What would you say," said Randolph, "if I told you that you just pointed exactly towards downtown Spokane and downtown Seattle? Or what's left of them, anyway."

"I would say that's really weird," I said.

"You get used to it," said Randolph.

"Why did I just point towards Seattle and Spokane?" I said.

"Because," said Randolph, "you are sensing the location of the nearest major gates. The static in your head is the presence of the Dark's hive mind. Castle Base is too far away from any active Darksiders for you to sense any individual creatures, but as you get closer, you would be able to detect them."

Maggie frowned. "You mean… he can detect the Dark?"

"That is correct, Miss Kane," said Randolph. He tapped the bronze microphone pin on his collar. "Mr. Kane, welcome to the Listeners."

Chapter 5

Training

I spent about ten days in Castle Base's infirmary recovering from the treatment.

After that, I didn't have another idle moment for about seven months.

Major Randolph gave me the rundown on what had happened to me as I recovered.

"I don't know how much your father told you about the Dark," he said.

"Not much," I said. "A little bit before he died. I didn't know about them until Invasion Day." We had already started calling it that.

Randolph nodded. "Not surprising. Daniel always took opsec seriously. Anyway, I'll tell you what they told me when I became a Listener. The first Darksiders started showing up in the 1950s, mostly coming out of very small gates located in rural places. We don't have any records of them before that, which is why the scientists think it was the first nuclear explosions that attracted them to Earth. The first recorded instance of a Dark gate is in Ukraine in 1953, and at the time the Soviets thought that it was something we had done, some kind of American superweapon in answer to the H-bomb. Then in 1954, Darksiders wiped out a village on a reservation in South

Dakota, and our government realized that the Soviets were not making these things up. President Eisenhower understood that the Dark was going to be a serious threat, and so he established the Black Division in the utmost secrecy. The Soviets did the same thing, more or less, and so did the Chinese and the other regional powers at the time."

"Okay," I said. Randolph had encouraged me to ask questions, so I was going to take him up on it. "Then I guess Black Division's mission was to fight the Dark?"

"That is correct," said Randolph. "Our official directive is to repulse any Darksider incursions, gather any and all knowledge about them, and serve as the nucleus around which a larger fighting force will be formed in the event of a full-scale invasion. Which, as you have probably guessed, has already happened."

"Another question," I said. "If we've known about the Dark for seventy years, why weren't we more ready to fight them?"

Randolph grimaced. "That is something of a sensitive topic. We've known an invasion was coming for decades, and officers from the Black Division have briefed every single President and Secretary of Defense over that time. Suffice it to say that the last few Presidents have been more interested in squandering money on foreign adventures and in building up the domestic bureaucracy than in actually doing anything likely to prove useful. Maybe the situation is different in other countries— I don't know. We don't have a clear idea of anything that's happening outside of North America at the moment. No one trusts anyone, and although we're in touch with various resistance groups, no one is telling anyone the truth. But that's beyond our present area of concern. Right now, we need to talk about what has happened to you."

"Okay," I said. "Why am I hearing things in my head?"

"As we fought Darksider raids over the last seventy years, we learned many things about them," said Randolph. "For one, their technology is entirely based on biological manipulation and genetic engineering, and they can do crazy things with it." He waved a hand at the infirmary. "If we wanted a building, we would have to build it. If the Dark wants a building, they code a seed with the appropriate genetic specifications and grow themselves a building."

"Suppose that saves on construction costs," I said.

"We don't think they use money," said Randolph, "or even understand the concept. They're a hive mind of some kind. The Darksiders you've encountered already, the ones that killed your father, those are just drones. They are basically organic computers programmed to hunt and kill. The more dangerous Darksiders are sapient, to some degree, and can communicate with us using language, but they're still a part of the hive mind."

"Is that what I'm hearing in my head?" I said. "The hive mind?"

"Exactly," said Randolph with a nod. "The Dark's biotech is very advanced by our standards, and permits them to commandeer other organic creatures in order to rewrite their nervous system. That joins them to the hive mind. After being brainjacked, the zombies become part of the Dark's hive mind, and it uses them as scouts, guards, cannon fodder, and so on."

"So I was supposed to become a zombie," I said.

"Yes," said Randolph. "Until about twenty-five years ago, there was no known cure. However, after the fall of the Soviet Union, Russia fell apart for a while, and for most of the 1990s the Russian government lost the ability to deal with the Dark effectively. A Russian oligarch named Mikhail Gregor took matters into his own hands…"

"Sorry. What's an oligarch?"

"In this context, a rich billionaire who is wealthy and powerful enough to put himself outside the law," said Randolph.

"I think I've heard of Gregor," I said. "My Dad used to talk about him. He said that Gregor was one of the top ten candidates to reveal himself as the Antichrist. He said Gregor was one of the chief architects of the New World Order, or the empire of the reptile people, or something."

"An exaggeration, to an extent, but more or less in keeping with Gregor's reputation," said Randolph. "He got his start supervising KGB prison facilities in central Asia. The man is, or was, I suppose, a nasty piece of work, and if things had gone differently he might well have become a dictator somewhere in one of the former Soviet republics. Anyway, he assembled his own private army to deal with incursions, then he started capturing Darksiders and experimenting on them. He thought there was money to be made by reverse-engineering their biotech. In the process, his scientists discovered a method for treating the conversion technology that created the zombies."

"Which saved me," I said.

"And me," said Randolph. "Gregor's treatment was an accident, but a useful one. What he wanted was a way to hack the Dark's conversion technology and use it as a targeted retrovirus for killing cancer cells. What he got was a method of hacking the biotech and putting it under the control of the conversion victim." He tapped his forehead. "That's why you and I are Listeners, Mr. Kane. We both have nervous systems and bloodstreams full of crippled Darkside biotech. It can't control us, but it still functions… which means we are still connected to the Dark's hive mind."

"That's… well, that's just creepy," I said.

Randolph smiled. "It is extremely creepy. I'm still not entirely used to it. That said, it's very useful. Our abilities let us detect the Dark, and over an extremely long range. In military terms, that is a tremendous advantage on both the strategic and tactical levels. We can hide from the Darksiders, but they cannot hide from us. Gregor gave his treatment to the Russian government to stay in the good side of the security services, and the Russian government shared the information with other governments that had active anti-Dark organizations. Black Division was one of them, of course, and that was when the Listener program started."

"So we're Listeners," I said. "People who can sense the Dark."

"We can sense Darksiders," said Randolph. "Perhaps more usefully, we can also sense their gates. That's the sharp feeling in your head. You're sensing the open gates in Spokane and Seattle. Specifically, you're sensing the transductor crystal they use to power the gates and keep them open. The crystals are alive and connected to the hive mind, so that's why we can sense them. The main role of the Listeners before Invasion Day was to find and destroy the gates so the Dark couldn't establish a beachhead. Now that we're at war, our primary role is reconnaissance and discovery. General Culver means to retake the entirety of the United States from them, and we've got an important role to play in that."

"So we're basically signals intelligence?" I said.

Randolph blinked. "More or less. I see your father taught you well. Look, I can promise you, you won't be bored. We need more Listeners than we have."

"When do I start?" I said.

"After you complete basic training," said Randolph, "when you're well enough."

Six days after that, the doctors pronounced me well enough to leave, and I went to basic training.

Boot camp was… I'm not going to say it was easy, because it wasn't. That said, while I did learn new things, I knew a lot of the stuff related to handling firearms and explosives already, thanks to Dad. The exercise was a challenge, yeah, but I just plowed on and kept at it. Learning to salute and navigate the rank hierarchy and obey without question wasn't hard either, since that was basically how Dad raised me and Maggie.

In the end, I would say boot camp was difficult but often boring, which as it turned out was a good preview of life as a soldier.

Except life as a Listener could got really dangerous and really weird. But more on that later.

Boot camp involved a lot of work and a lot of exercise and taking orders, so I'll skip over most of it. Our instructor was Drill Sergeant Lawson, and despite what you see in movies, he never swore, he never insulted anyone, and he only raised his voice to make sure that his orders were heard by everyone in the training company. That said, the man was a harsh taskmaster, and failure or laxness of any kind was punished by lots of pushups, or long runs, or cleaning the barracks latrines, or his personal favorite, pushups followed by running followed by cleaning the barracks latrines.

I did that one a couple of times.

There were a lot of recruits in Castle Base during those months. I didn't know it at the time, but Invasion Day had destroyed the federal government and the upper tiers of the military, and General Culver was essentially acting as an independent warlord. He had taken control of most of Washington and Oregon east of the Cascades (west of the Cascades belonged to the Dark), all of Idaho, and big chunks of Montana, Wyoming, and Nevada. Evidently the Mormon Church had taken control of Utah and most of Colorado after destroying the Darkside gate that had opened in Temple Square. Dad did always say that the Mormons had a lot of guns. The Mormons had their own independent state now, but no military, so they had allied with General Culver, since he and the officers of Black Division were the only people in the country who had any idea what was going on, even though the General was some kind of Baptist or another.

Whoever was in charge of the Mormons decreed that it was a religious duty for every young Mormon male to fight alien invaders in lieu of a missionary trip, and so thousands of them turned up to join General Culver's army. I think my training company might have been the most clean-cut and orderly one in the history of the United States. The Mormons were friendly, and I got along well enough with them, but I wasn't a Mormon and didn't have any interest in becoming one, so I never really became friends with any of them.

Then once I finished boot camp, I got rotated into a different, much smaller training company.

It was training for Listeners. People like me, in other words.

We weren't nearly so clean-cut. Black Division didn't have as many Listeners as it needed because Listeners were very hard to create. First a victim had to be exposed to the Dark's conversion weapon, and then the victim had to be treated within a specific window of time, else the conversion would complete and instead of a Listener the Dark would have a new zombie. Adding to the risk was the fact that the treatment had a fifty percent mortality rate. Even so, when the Division captured samples of the conversion weapon, a few men volunteered to become Listeners. Major Randolph was one of them.

That said, the Division got most of its Listeners from those who had survived zombie attacks. Before Invasion Day, if the Dark attacked an isolated area, there were often survivors, and sometimes the Division arrived in time to rescue people and treat them. Those who survived became Listeners. After Invasion Day, there were far more victims, which meant a lot more opportunities to create Listeners. Like me.

My squad had five men in it, counting myself. The next oldest after me was an eighteen-year-old soldier from Georgia named Rufus Archibald Bullock the Fifth, and he had enlisted in the United States Army seven months before. I think he was the only one who was actually excited to become a Listener. When I met him, he enthusiastically started to inform me of his lineage.

"My dad fought in Iraq," he said. "His dad fought in Vietnam. His dad fought in the Pacific against the Japanese, and his dad fought the Spanish in Cuba…"

"Guess it runs in the family, then," I said.

He grinned and pumped my hand. He wasn't doing that thing where he tried to crush my hand, but he was strong. "Call me Bull. Everyone does."

"Can't imagine why," I said, and Bull brayed with laughter. He was a big dude. If he played football in high school, any coach with two brain cells to rub together would have put him in the defensive line, and Bull would have sacked the quarterback two or three times every game.

"I think we're blessed, you know?" said Bull.

"Sorry?" I said. I supposed we were lucky to be alive, but I hadn't thought of it in those terms.

"The thing we've got in our heads, it's a gift," said Bull. "It's a gift from God. This war is a righteous war to defend all of mankind, and God will be on our side. We are blessed indeed. Other men who have fought in wars had to fight other men. We get to fight monsters, and that does not weigh upon our consciences."

"I suppose not," I said. Bull sometimes got in trouble for trying to evangelize to the Mormons, but he and I always got along. He was really excited about killing lots and lots of Darksiders, and I could get behind that.

I also got along with Jack. His real name was John Walter, which made him sound like the managing partner of a law firm, but he was actually a cop. Specifically, he was twenty-nine years old, and he had been a Seattle cop for six years. When the gates opened in Seattle, he and four other men from the Seattle police department had kept their heads together and escorted something like five hundred civilians into the countryside once it became obvious that the city was lost. On the other side of the Cascades, they were attacked by a band of drones and zombies. They fought off the Dark, and while Jack had made it, his four friends did not. A patrol from Castle Base came across the scene in time to give Jack the treatment, and he had become one of the Listeners.

"Your dad was a law enforcement officer?" said Jack when we first met. He talked exactly like a cop. He was a former "law enforcement officer", not a cop. He never went anywhere, he "proceeded" to places. When describing crimes and situations, he had a tendency to use police codes, and then needed to translate them to English. He also had an uncanny ability to exactly guess someone's height and weight when meeting them.

"Yeah," I said. "He was in the Division before Invasion Day went down, so he was clued in about the Dark."

"I'm sorry," said Jack. "I didn't have a family—my dad died when I was a kid, and my mom a couple years after I joined the department. Heart attacks, both of them."

"Sorry about that," I said.

We stood in silence for a moment.

"Well," said Jack with a sudden smile, "given my family's history of Code Blues, I suppose I should have picked a less stressful job."

"Ha," I said. "If those zombies didn't give you a heart attack, then nothing will."

My dad once said that in every group of ten men, there were two leaders, seven followers, and one troublemaker. I think he was quoting some old-time general or another, but if that general was right, then Jack was our natural leader. He became the leader of his squad by default. It wasn't so much that he told us what to do, but he helped make sure that we had what we needed to do it.

And if Jack was a natural leader, then Tong was one of nature's followers.

His full name was Nguyen Tran Tong, and his grandparents and parents were Vietnamese immigrants who had settled in Los Angeles after fleeing from the Communists back in the 70s. His extended family had enough experience with war and displacement to see the writing on the wall when the Darkside gates opened in LA, and they had gotten out of town before everything got really nasty. Somewhere in Nevada, the Nguyen family had been attacked by zombies, and they had been on the verge of getting overwhelmed when one of the Division's patrols had found them.

Tong had made it. His parents had not, and once he survived the treatment he joined Black Division as a Listener.

Don't get me wrong—when I say Tong was a follower, that's not an insult. He was good at, well, everything, and he could field-strip and rebuild his rifle faster than I could manage, and I had way more experience with firearms. He was an absolute genius at organization and planning. That said, I think Mama Nguyen was a bit of a tyrant. Tong tended not to do anything unless he had been explicitly told to do it. Fortunately, Jack liked to tell people what to do, so he and Tong got along well.

If Tong was one of nature's followers, then the last member of our squad was one of nature's troublemakers.

I never managed to figure out Nate Rigger's ethnicity, and he didn't volunteer information about himself. He was twenty-five years old, and to judge from his tattoos and some of his passing remarks, he had escaped from prison when the Dark had overrun the complex. He might have been Hispanic, or he might have been a Caucasian who had spent a lot of time in the sun. He was surly and argumentative, and he had a cruel, nasty streak, but he had survived the zombies, so he was a Listener. In less desperate times, the Division would never have taken him because of his tendency to settle problems through violence, but there was a war on and Rigger was a Listener.

And he didn't like me on sight.

I didn't know why and he never did tell me. In hindsight, I think it was because I was the youngest one in the group, and whatever governed the buzzing mass of violent impulses that served as Rigger's brain decided I would make a likely target. Rigger embarked on a campaign of petty harassment—tying my bootlaces together, hiding my gear so I would get in trouble, that kind of thing. He also never hesitated to shove me into the nearest wall, so long as no one was watching.

After about two weeks of that, I decided it was time to take action.

We were walking back to the barracks after class, and Rigger gave me a shove that sent me stumbling. I caught my balance, gave him a big sunny smile, and then hit him in the nose. Palm strike, open-handed, and the shock of the impact went all the way up my arm. Dad had been very clear about protecting your knuckles in physical combat.

Rigger staggered back, dark eyes wide with shock, blood streaming from his nose, then bellowed and came at me.

It turned out to be about an even match. Rigger was bigger and had considerably more practical experience of violence, but I had the benefit of Dad's lessons, I was in better shape, and I kept my head better. He might have survived prison, but I'd killed my share of men and Darksiders. We wound up rolling around on the grass, grappling for leverage and landing whatever blows we could. I took a pretty good elbow to the head, but I caught him with a knee to the stomach just before we were wrenched apart by others. I got to my feet, but my head was still spinning, and I took a step backward before falling on my backside.

Rigger sat up, glaring daggers at me. "I'm gonna crack your head open like…"

He paused, blinked, and held up one finger, then turned his head and threw up his breakfast. Guess my knee had hit him hard.

"Okay," he said. "Now I'm gonna…"

He turned his head and puked again, and I started to laugh.

Rigger glared at me once he'd finished. "What? What's so funny?"

"It's not," I said, "but you can't crack my head open if you keep throwing up."

Rigger stared at me in confusion, then he made a wheezing noise. I thought he was going to puke again, but the wheezing sound kept coming, and I realized that he was laughing.

I wasn't sure what was funny, but it was so absurd that I started laughing too.

"Yeah," croaked Rigger. "Yeah, guess I can't."

And then he laughed again. Just like that, he stopped giving me trouble. We still didn't like each other, but he didn't give me grief anymore.

That incident also helped me figure out my place in the squad. Remember what I said about the natural leaders and followers and troublemakers?

It turns out that everyone saw me as the squad psycho. I followed all the rules to the letter. I really enjoyed using firearms, and I knew more about them than everyone else in the squad, even Jack and Bull. I didn't really have much of a sense of humor, except at inappropriate times. And even Rigger didn't give me trouble, and if Rigger didn't give a guy trouble, you knew he had to be dangerous. I got along with everyone, but they were a little afraid of me.

Because I had become the squad's psycho.

I didn't mind. I supposed I really was Daniel Kane's son, and I bet he had been the squad psycho wherever he went. And while I didn't think I was a psychopath, I knew I wasn't normal. I had shot that guy who tried to grab Maggie without hesitation and without regret. Granted, he had probably deserved shooting even before the invasion, but I think most people would have felt something when shooting a man for the first time.

I didn't, and that didn't bother me. Because if God and Daniel Kane had made me into a killer, then I was going to kill a whole lot of Darksiders.

After appropriate classroom instruction, of course.

Major Randolph and a few other officers who were Listeners taught the class. There were classes on tactics and strategy and on the history of signals intelligence, which made sense as we were basically living signals intelligence assets. I supposed the classes on strategy and tactics were to help us interpret whatever information we picked up from the Dark.

"The central problem of being a Listener," said Randolph, standing in front of the little classroom where we met, "is that you are now essentially a modified human, a hybrid of sorts. You are tapping into the Dark's hive mind, and the human mind has not evolved to handle those kind of sensations–"

"God created the Heavens and the Earth in six days, sir," said Bull.

"Don't interrupt," said Randolph.

"Sir," said Bull.

"Whether evolution or God or aliens from the Dog Star made the human mind," continued Randolph, "the fact remains that your brain is not equipped to interpret a connection to an alien hive mind. It interprets the connection to the hive mind in the context of sensations with which you are already familiar. Fortunately, we have seen a uniformity of response among the Listeners. The purpose of this class is to teach you how to better understand those sensations so that you can utilize them for combat purposes."

Major Randolph and the other Listener officers had a PowerPoint.

It turned out to be a long PowerPoint.

The first thing we learned about was how to sense the presence of the gates. That one was easy. We could feel the presence of the big gates in Spokane and Seattle, and Randolph explained that our brains were sensing the presence of the transductor crystals the Dark used to force open the portals from their world or dimension or wherever they came from. Our brains interpreted the presence of a transductor as a sensation of pressure, and as we gained experience, we would learn to gauge the distance and size of the gates.

"That is our most vital task, closing the gates," said Randolph. "Black Division means to drive back the enemy and retake first the United States and then the world, and we're going to do that by closing the enemy's gates one by one."

"How can a gate be closed, sir?" asked Jack.

"At present, the only known way is to send a team through the gate and to the Dark's home world," said Randolph. "Once through the gate, they need to locate the transductor crystal powering the gate and carry it with them back through the gate to Earth. That causes the gate to immediately collapse. As you can imagine, the Dark guards their transductor crystals quite well." He looked the classroom over. "The long-term strategic goal is to close as many gates as possible and to study their transductor crystals until we understand how to block them. That will be our path to victory in this war. Black Division's original mandate was to defend mankind against the Dark's incursions, but as we have seen, that reactive and defensive philosophy proved insufficient. The mandate has changed. General Culver and the rest of our leadership will now accept nothing less than total victory over the Dark, and that is the goal of each and every man in this room."

We spent a lot of time studying the different sensations that different kinds of Darksiders would produce in us. Generally, the presence of Darksiders produced a sensation that felt like water droplets against the skin, and if the Darksider was an Overseer or other sapient form, the temperature of the sensation would rise. If we got close enough, we could even hear the Darksiders speaking to each other within the hive mind. Unfortunately, it wasn't quite like listening in on a phone call. The Darksiders didn't use language to communicate with each other, but rather a continual flow of data, and there was no way of decoding it that we knew about.

Once we finished basic training, there was a little ceremony. Major Randolph gave a speech, and then we had a dinner. Maggie was there, and I was pleased to see that she was doing well at Castle Base. She had been working in the central offices between her classes at the base's school. Dad had always said that the Army was like the DMV but with more guns in terms of paperwork, and Black Division was still the same.

I was also pleased to learn that General Culver didn't have any interest in recruiting female combat troops, which meant I didn't have to worry about Maggie getting drafted and sent into battle. I suppose his opinion had been out-of-step with modern times, but after the Dark had wiped out two-thirds of the human race on Invasion Day, his position on the matter made rather more sense.

We had finished basic training, but that was one thing. Actually sensing the presence of the Dark out in the field was something else entirely. New Listeners were sent out with veteran troops on combat patrols to practice our skills until we mastered them.

Which was how I found myself in my first battle.

Chapter 6

First Mission

The man in charge of my first combat patrol was named Captain Jonas Howard.

Captain Howard had been in Afghanistan and Iraq, which he was willing to talk about, and some other places that he was not. He spoke in a slow Alabama drawl, rarely raising his voice, and constantly chewed sunflower seeds as a means of keeping nicotine addiction at bay. He had learned the truth about the Dark the same way that so many others in Black Division had—on patrol outside Kandahar, a hole ripping itself in the air, and then a horde of giant stinking alien bug-things swarming out to kill everything in sight.

Or so Captain Howard put it. He had bit of a flair for the dramatic.

Bull and I reported to Captain Howard's HQ as ordered at 0500 one dark, dry morning. Howard's HQ was a large tent with a space heater, since Castle Base had gotten a bit crowded since Invasion Day. I had heard rumors that Black Division had facilities elsewhere, and that General Culver was taking in more regular Army bases under his command, but I hadn't visited any of them yet.

Howard stood outside his tent, watching as his men loaded up their armored troop carriers. There were already a dozen sunflower seed shells around his boots. If he wasn't careful he was going to need dentures by the time he turned fifty, assuming any of us lived that long.

"Sir!" I said. "Corporal Roland Kane and Corporal Rufus Bullock reporting for duty, sir!"

We saluted. Howard sized us up, then saluted back after a moment.

I should have mentioned that. Listeners started at corporal rank, since in the heat of combat we sometimes had to tell privates to move quickly to avoid a Darkside attack.

"You two look too young to be corporals," grunted Howard. He pointed at me. "You don't look old enough to drive."

"I am seventeen years old, sir!" I announced. My birthday had passed while in basic training. Maggie had scraped together enough flour to make me a cupcake, which had been nice.

"Don't shout unless I tell you," said Howard. "Some of those drones have ears like bats. Let me guess. You got bit by a zombie, the Division found you in time, and now you're a Listener?"

"Yes, sir," I said.

Howard's gaze shifted to Bull. "And you. You're a big fellow, aren't you?"

"Yes, sir!" said Bull with enthusiasm. "I am excited for the opportunity to bring destruction upon the Dark, sir!"

"You're not bringing destruction to anyone," said Howard. "You're staying in the vehicles. The General himself will rip me a new one if I get one of his Listeners killed."

"Yes, sir!" said Bull. "Then I am excited for the opportunity to bring destruction to the Dark vicariously, sir!"

Howard blinked and his lips twitched. I suspect he almost laughed. "Let's hope you can retain that enthusiasm, Corporal. Both of you, report to Sergeant Mendez and do whatever he tells you."

"Yes, sir," Bull and I chorused in unison.

Sergeant Mendez turned out to be a Hispanic man in his middle thirties with a scarred face and tattoos that were occasionally visible when he took off his jacket. He looked like an enforcer for a drug gang, but he ran a tight ship. I suspect the fact that he looked like he could murder you with his bare hands without blinking helped him keep order.

"All right, you two," said Mendez. "You'll be with me in the second carrier." He pointed at the second of the six M200 armored personnel carriers that would make up our patrol. "You're new, so shut up, keep your ears peeled, and do your thing. You detect even a hint of Darksiders, you speak up right away, got it?"

"Yes, sir," Bull and I said in unison.

"There's going to be trouble on this patrol, so stay sharp," said Mendez.

"How do you know there will be trouble, Sergeant?" I said.

"General said so," said Mendez.

By now I had realized that most of the men of Black Division regarded General Culver as something like a prophet. It was well-known within the Division that Culver had been trying to warn Washington and the Pentagon about the Dark for years, and that he had been warning them something like Invasion Day was going to happen sooner or later. The Pentagon had ignored his warning, save for occasional demands to increase the number of female combat troops in the Division.

Well, General Culver had been proven right. It also helped that he seemed to be one of the few powerful people left with an actual plan other than hiding in a bunker someplace and hoping that his canned soup didn't run out. And he had won the loyalty of someone like my father, and Dad hated everyone.

"Will we run into the GDC, Sergeant?" said Bull.

Mendez grunted. It sounded like a negative, but it was hard to be sure. I wasn't about to ask for clarification.

The GDC was one of the potential problems we might encounter. General Culver was a man with a plan... but there were other men with other plans, and some of them had formed a group called the Global Defense Committee, which we usually just called the GDC. The GDC controlled most of northern Mexico, nearly all of California, and a big chunk of the Southwest. No one knew much about them, but rumor held that they consisted of former California National Guard officers, former Mexican army generals, the heads of several drug cartels, and even a Silicon Valley billionaire.

General Culver might have found himself a warlord, but he was a warlord with a vision. Nor did he permit misbehavior in his troops. A couple of soldiers had been executed for murdering and robbing or otherwise molesting civilians, and the General had made it very clear our mission was to defend the people of the United States, not to terrorize them.

The GDC viewed things differently. According to the reports, they made a habit of using terror and intimidation to keep the local populations in line, including crucifixion and throwing people off roofs and burning them alive and various other techniques that had been perfected in the Middle East in the last ten years or so before Invasion Day. Early on, they had tried to bring the territory protected by the Black Division under their control, and the Division had inflicted such a sharp defeat on them that the Committee hadn't tried to make any trouble for General Culver since.

It wasn't just the defeat that kept the peace, though. Both the Division and the Committee had their hands full with the Dark; the Darkside base in Las Vegas was a particular thorn in the Committee's side. Rumors that the GDC was going to try to ally with us, or attack us, were common, but none of them proved to be anything but scuttlebutt.

"Naw," said Mendez at last. "We're too far north for that. The General thinks the Dark are due to make some trouble. Spokane's their last stronghold on this side of the Cascades, and he thinks they'll try to break out. If we find them, we shut them down. If we run into too many of them, we call for reinforcements. Now get into the vehicle and listen for trouble."

With that cheery thought, Bull and I climbed into Mendez's M200. That lasted all of thirty seconds, when Howard radioed Mendez and told him to send one of the Listeners to his vehicle, since that way both Listeners wouldn't get blown up if someone shot our carrier. Mendez told Bull to join Howard, and he obeyed with alacrity.

Then we set off.

Our patrol started off heading north along the old U.S. Highway 195, but soon we turned west and headed off the road into the deserts of eastern Washington. The Dark sometimes used the roads to move their land-based forces, but they just as often abandoned the roads to travel cross-country, so we had to do the same. The deserts were pretty in a stark, austere kind of way, with a lot of rocky hills and a lot of scrubby little bushes. The M200s made good time over the uneven ground, and I listened to the radio chatter from the other vehicles, as Howard or Mendez ordered one gunner to cover various angles or discussed what approach to take through a valley. From time to time we stopped and checked our position via GPS. I wondered how much longer the GPS network would keep working. The satellites were still in orbit, but sooner or later they would fail, and there might not be a government left with the resources to replace them.

There might not be any people left on Earth by then.

I put that thought out of my head. General Culver and Major Randolph and every other officer I had encountered had strong words about defeatism and the evils they would inflict upon anyone caught up by such an unsoldierly vice.

Then my head started to feel wet, as if water droplets were striking my face.

It was bone-dry inside the M200.

I tapped the sergeant's shoulder. He ordered the driver to stop and told me to check in with Bull.

I grabbed my radio. "Bull, this is Kane. You getting that?"

"Yeah," said Bull, a bit of excitement in his voice. "Yeah, I was just about to call you. What do you think? About three miles north of here?"

"I think so," I said. "Else we would have detected them before now."

"What and where, corporals?" Howard demanded.

"Darksiders inbound, sir," I said. "Twenty or thirty drones, I think. There's at least one Overseer with them, too."

"Speed and direction?" said Howard.

"Heading south right at us, sir," said Bull. "It feels like they're in a hurry, sir."

"I think we're right in their path," I added.

"Roger," said Howard. "Good work. Sergeant, a word."

Mendez leaned over and switched his radio to his private channel with the captain. I could hear Mendez's half of the conversation, and it sounded as if they were planning a tactical maneuver.

"All right," the captain announced to all of us once they'd finished their little conference. "This is what we're going to do." He rapidly issued a series of orders, and the column broke up. Four of the M200s parked themselves in the Dark's path, right in the middle of a little valley, spaced out so the enemy couldn't kill us all if they had explosives handy. The gunners swung the machine guns to point to the north. Two of our vehicles climbed the hilltops on either side of the valley to provide covering fire. Both of those M200s had mortar teams, and Howard wanted the weapons sighted at the mouth of the valley. The troops all knew their business, and it wasn't long before we were all in position.

"Good to go, sir," said Mendez.

"Excellent," said Howard. "Listeners?"

I closed my eyes and concentrated. "They should be in visual range in about 60 seconds."

"All troops be ready to fire at my command," said Howard. "Anyone fires early, I'll volunteer him for the Listeners."

Acknowledgments came over the channel. I felt a sudden eerie whispering in my head, like murmurs too quiet to catch. I was close enough to the Darksiders that I could pick up the communications of the local node of their hive mind, even though I couldn't understand what they were saying.

"Visual!" someone said over the radio.

I saw the Darksiders on the monitor, stark and sharp upon the M200's cameras. There were about thirty of the giant locust-like drones, similar to the ones that I had seen in Chicago on Invasion Day, but these were almost the size of horses. Their bladed forelimbs were as long as my leg, and if they managed to close with us, they could slaughter everyone in short order.

An Overseer was behind them.

Overseers look vaguely humanoid, albeit encased in obsidian-like chitin, though they have four legs instead of two, and you need to take off at least three of the legs before they stop moving. Their heads are a ghastly combination of insect, squid, and something with no earthly equivalent, and they're tough. Their carapaces can shrug off small-arms fire, and sometimes they can even keep fighting after a direct grenade hit.

Worse than that, they're smart. Give me a strong but dumb enemy over a smart but weak one any day of the week, and the Overseers are both strong and smart. We think the Overseers are sapient, but they all seem to be in harmony with the hive mind. Despite that, they can take initiative and plan independently, and they had a bad habit of setting nasty traps for us.

That said, it didn't seem like this particular Overseer was all that smart. It was driving the drones forward, running behind them with great haste. It must have been in a hurry to get somewhere. As it approached, the sensation of their presence in my head shifted, and I looked up. That was stupid—all I saw was the riveted metal ceiling of the M200. But the presence of the Dark abruptly shifted in my head.

"Sergeant," I said. "There are flyers incoming."

"I got them," said Bull. "Maybe twenty drones. They're about sixty seconds behind the ground units."

"Then let's take the groundpounders out first," said Howard. "Open fire!"

For a moment, nothing happened. Then I heard a faint whistling noise, followed by two dull thumps as the mortars landed in the midst of the charging drones and exploded. The scout drones came to a confused halt as their Overseer spotted us, and the other M200s opened up with their machine guns. We were all wearing electronic ear protectors as part of our helmets and radio headsets, which was a good thing because those guns were loud. Sitting in a M200 with a machine gun firing from its roof felt like sitting in an oil drum that was being used as an actual drum.

Fortunately, the guns were just as effective as they were loud. Streams of machine gun fire ripped across the drones, mowing them down like grass. The Overseer stumbled as several rounds hit it, but the creature managed to get something that looked like a long black oval up to its shoulder.

"Energy weapon!" I said. "Overseer has an energy weapon! I repeat, the Overseer has an energy weapon!"

"Take it down!" said Mendez. "Gunners two, three, get it!"

Two of the gunners turned the full fury of their machine guns on the Overseer. The stream of high-caliber bullets turned the Overseer into glistening black pulp, but not before it got off a shot from its weapon. Those energy weapons used some sort of hyper-accelerated plasma. I had seen a description in training, but I'm not a scientist and I don't understand how it works. What I did know was that a blast of reddish-white fire came from the weapon and hurtled towards our M200.

The driver was on the ball, and the vehicle lurched forward. The bolt that would have hit us head on instead clipped the side of the M200. The vehicle rang like a bell. Some of the displays on the walls and the driver station went dead, and the temperature went up by about thirty degree in a second.

I smelled burnt plastic and hot metal. I was afraid that the plasma blast had hit the fuel tank and we were all about to go up in a fireball. But then the M200 stopped shaking.

We had survived the hit. The impact had given me a headache, though, and I felt a steadily building pressure inside my head.

"Aerial inbound!" shouted the driver.

"Anti-air, anti-air!" said Mendez and Howard almost simultaneously.

The tone of the machine gun fire changed as the gunners started shooting skyward. I heard a thump as a dead scout drone bounced off the side of the vehicle, and then more thumps as several dead scout drones hit the ground.

Then a clang, and suddenly sunlight stabbed into the interior of the M200.

A scout drone wrenched open the hatch on the roof, and it started to thrust itself into the vehicle. I saw the sunlight glint off its armored carapace, saw its mouthparts twitching and its multiple banks of antennae swaying back and forth like grass in a breeze. Every other man in the vehicle was fully occupied with their tasks. It suddenly occurred to me that being locked in a big metal can being opened by a Darksider was a great way to get carved to bloody chunks.

Fortunately, I already had my weapon in hand. I raised it, flipping the selector switch to full auto and squeezing the trigger in one smooth motion. I sent a burst of fire through the drone, turning its head to black pulp, and the twitching body fell to the deck.

"Secure that hatch!" roared Mendez. One of the gunners hurried forward, seized the hatch, and swung it shut with another clang. Mendez pointed at me. "Kane, report."

"I think we've got them all, sergeant," I said, frowning. Confirmation was coming over the radio. But the pressure in my head was still growing. "Bull, you getting this?" No answer. "Bull, respond please."

"Yeah," said Bull, his voice thick. "Sorry. Distracted. Uh, the pressure in my head? You getting that too?"

"I think a gate's about to open," I said.

Mendez swore. "Captain, you hear that?"

"I did," said Howard. "Corporal Kane, Corporal Bullock, location?"

"About two miles south of here, I think," I said.

"Agreed," said Bull. "But there's something off about it."

"Go on," ordered Howard.

I frowned, remembering what I had learned from Major Randolph in training, about how to interpret the various sensations that came with being a Listener.

"I think, sir," I said. "I think the gate hasn't opened yet. I think it's about to open."

"Agreed, sir," said Bull. "It feels like the gate is about to open, but it's not all the way there yet."

"Then we have ourselves an opportunity," said Howard. "Damage reports, quickly. I want to be headed south in two minutes."

Status reports came over the radio channel. Our APC was the only one that had taken any damage, and the plasma blast had only clipped the M200, shearing off some of the armor but not damaging any of the vehicle's systems. The APC was still in fighting shape, though it would be vulnerable to any fire that hit the rear right quarter. The other six vehicles had come through without any damage, and still had enough ammunition for another fight.

"All right," said Howard. "Kane, Bullock. Due south?"

"Ah," I said, scrambling to examine the map and my compass, trying to triangulate the direction from the weird sensations in my skull. "Yes, sir. Directly south."

"Straight south, sir," said Bull.

"Move out," said Howard. "I want spotters watching our path. If the enemy is opening a gate, we should see waste light generated by the process. I repeat, all spotters are to watch for waste light from the enemy gate."

The M200 rumbled back into motion, swinging down to the south, and I saw the other vehicles following suit. We drove south across the desert, and I felt the pressure in my head increase. The gate was opening, but I didn't think it was all the way open yet.

"Least we know where that patrol was going in such a hurry, sir," said Mendez. "Probably coming here to secure that gate."

"Almost certainly," said Howard. "Listeners. Can you tell how large the gate is going to be?"

"I'm not sure, sir," I said. "I don't think it's going to be very large, though. Maybe big enough for one of the APCs to drive through, sir."

"Nothing like the gates at Spokane or the other major cities, sir," added Bull.

"Scout gate, then," said Howard. "They've been using those lately, dropping small forces in friendly territory to cause trouble. Command thinks that the Dark might have a hard limit on their capacity to maintain open gates, and most of that capacity is tied up in the major cities."

"Sir," said Mendez. "This might be a chance to capture another transductor crystal."

"I was just thinking that, Sergeant," said Howard. "If we play our cards right, we might drive home with a crystal to present to the General's scientists. They love the wretched things."

"Sir," said one of the spotters. "Gate spotted up ahead."

"Is it open yet?" said Howard.

"No, sir," said the spotter.

Even over the radio, I heard the satisfaction in Captain Howard's voice, and I did see Mendez smile. Mendez hardly ever smiled, which made it rather unsettling. I looked at the monitors as the cameras focused on a patch of desert a few hundred meters ahead of us. A sheet of mist and gray light rippled there, and the pressure on my skull was coming from that sheet of mist.

"What do you think?" said Howard. "Two minutes? Maybe three?"

"Two and a half at most," said Mendez.

"Listeners?" said Howard.

"It's going to open at any moment, sir," I said, and Bull agreed.

"Excellent." I heard the satisfaction in Howard's voice. "Gentlemen, God must love us, because he's dropped this gate gift-wrapped into our laps. Close to within fifty meters of the gate. Mortar teams and gunners, target the gate, and be ready to fire into it at my command."

"We're going to fire into the gate, sir?" I said.

"That's right," said Mendez. "We got lucky. Best way to deal with these gates is to be sitting in front of them when they open with a lot of fire. We shoot into the gate and wipe out the advance party. Then we're going to go through, kill the Overseers guarding the transductor crystal, and get out of there." He paused, then nodded at me. "Nice work, boys. You Listeners actually come in handy sometimes."

"Thank you, sir!" said Bull with unfeigned enthusiasm.

"How long until the gate opens?" said Howard.

"Less than a minute, sir," I said. "Any second now."

"Mortars, fire at my command," said Howard. "Missile launchers as well." A few of the soldiers had shoulder-fired missile launchers, and they had taken cover on the roofs of our APCs, ready to add their firepower to those of the mortar operators. I stared at the display, watching as the rippling curtain of mist grew brighter and brighter.

I felt the gate open before I saw it.

The pressure in my forehead intensified, and the mist blazed with white light that dimmed into gray as the gate opened. As it did, I felt the presence of more Darksiders on the other side of the gate even as I saw their eerie world on the other side, a hellish place with red skies and a landscape of huge, twisted mushrooms that glowed with purplish light.

There were a lot of Darksiders on the other side of the gate, a whole troop of scout drones, several Overseers, and a half-dozen assault drones. The assault drones were about the size of oxen, and looked like heavily armored beetles with tentacles and long, sharp pincers. Assault drones were strong, well-built, and they could get up to speeds of forty miles an hour on a flat stretch of terrain.

But they couldn't outrun a mortar blast.

"Fire!" said Howard.

Six mortar rounds and four shoulder-fired rockets streaked towards the gate. The Darksiders started to come out in a black wave, only to be met by a lethal quantity of explosives.

The blasts were impressive. The gate disappeared behind a massive spray of dirt and fire, as bits and pieces of Darksider chitin went flying high into the air.

"Gunners!" said Mendez. "Get the stragglers!"

The machine guns opened up, the gunners concentrating their fire on any Darksider that had escaped the initial barrage. The guns mowed down the surviving scout drones, and then joined fire to rip apart an assault drone that staggered free from the dust. An Overseer staggered forward, missing a leg and seemingly stunned by the violent ambush, and it aimed a plasma weapon in our direction, but the machine guns killed it before it could even get off a shot. A cheer went up over the radio as it collapsed, dead, onto the ground.

Then the firing stopped. I wondered for a moment if the gunners had run out of ammunition, but then I realized nothing else was emerging from the gate.

If this was a scout gate, then we had killed the entire scouting party waiting on the other side.

"Listeners?" said Howard. "What's out there?"

I concentrated hard on the gate, trying to focus on it. It was a peculiar sensation. I could sense the pressure of the gate, and I realized that I could also sense things on the other side of the gate. I could feel the presence of additional Darksiders on the far side of the gate, but they were at least a couple of miles off.

For a moment, the way was clear, and I could sense the sharp presence of the transductor on the other side of the gate.

"I think we got them all, sir," said Bull, and I concurred. "We've got a few minutes before more show up on the other side."

"Good," said Howard. "Mendez, take one of the M200s and one of the Listeners and get that transductor crystal."

"Yes, sir," said Mendez. Since I was already in his APC, I supposed that meant I was going with him. "Driver, take us through."

The driver gunned the engine, and the M200 rolled towards the gate.

"Kane," said Mendez. "You ever been on the other side of one of these things?"

"No, sir," I said. "This is my first time."

"Well, isn't this just your lucky day." Mendez smiled wryly. "Welcome to Hell."

The M200 rumbled towards the gate, and a second later it was through.

We had entered the world of the Dark. Or their planet, or plane, or dimension, or level of reality, or whatever the scientists wanted to call it this week. Even when seen from the other side of the gates, it looked horrifying.

Seen from the inside, it looked a whole lot worse.

We were in a jungle of giant black mushrooms, their greasy surfaces covered with veins that glowed with purple-black light, vines hanging from the underside of their caps like twisting serpents. The sky overhead was red, the color of blood, and filled with billowing thunderheads, black lightning leaping from cloud to cloud. In the distance, I saw a row of mountains, their slopes covered with glittering structures fashioned out of something that looked like obsidian.

Yet the sight was nothing compared to the ominous presence of the Dark inside my head.

I could feel them all around me, a tidal wave of sensations breaking against my skull. This whole planet was ruled by them, and even those giant mushroom things were somehow part of the hive mind. I could hear the whispers of the hive mind communicating with itself, but here, right in the heart of its power, I could practically make out what it was saying. I got the impression of a vast, insect-like thing planning a dozen different wars at once, and I could tell that the alien mind knew we were here.

I wobbled a little in my seat and grabbed at the wall to keep from falling over.

"You okay, corporal?" said Mendez.

"Yeah," I muttered. I forced myself to focus. "I mean, yes, sergeant. Bit of shock is all."

"The transductor is right ahead, sir," said one of the soldiers watching the monitors.

I looked at the display. Dead ahead rose a black, glistening thing that looked kind of like a corpse flower, if corpse flowers could grow to the size of minivans. Above its center floated a black crystal about the size of a volleyball, its facets flashing and flickering with harsh gray light. For reasons that the scientists had so far been unable to discern, transductor crystals had either thirty-six, forty-eight, or ninety-six facets, yet their size and complexity seemed to have nothing to do with the size of the gate they opened.

"Kane," said Mendez as the APC rolled to a stop by the glistening flower-thing. "How long do we have?"

"About four minutes, tops," I said.

"Let's move, people," said Mendez, lifting his rifle.

The door opened, and four soldiers got out. I followed them, my own gun in hand, and Mendez and two more soldiers came next. I jogged to the flower and slung my weapon over my shoulder, freeing my hands to carry the transductor crystal.

Then I reached up and plucked the crystal out of the air.

Anyone could touch one of the crystals. That said, occasionally touching the crystal caused a sudden link to the Dark's hive mind. The Listeners were used to that, and it didn't bother us much. But the shock could kill an unprepared soldier, so the job of carrying the transductor crystal fell to me.

It was heavier than it looked, about the weight of a bowling ball or so. A jolt went through me as I gripped the thing, and even through my gloves, it felt icy cold and hot at the same time. That was probably my brain trying to interpret the sensations it was picking up. The hive mind seemed to snap into focus around me, and I could almost understand the communications between the Darksiders around me. Their emotions were alien and strange, but undeniably malevolent. The hive mind hated humans, hated life, hated anything that was not a part of itself, and it desired to devour all other living things and leave itself alone and supreme in the universe. I could hear the whispers as the Darksiders rushed towards the site of the scout gate, preparing to kill us before we could steal the transductor crystal.

And the crystal itself…

I could hear it in my head. I think it was trying to talk to me. Unlike the Dark, it wasn't alive. I think it was a kind of machine, although a machine with a degree of sentience. I think it wanted me to use it, to do something with it, but I didn't know what. I frowned at the crystal, trying to understand what it was telling me.

"Corporal!"

I blinked and saw Mendez staring at me while the soldiers scanned the giant mushrooms for any foes.

"You still with us, corporal?" said Mendez.

"Yes, sir," I said. The whispers in my head were getting louder. "Sir, we should probably get out of here. Reinforcements are coming."

"Move out!" shouted Mendez, and the soldiers jogged back to the relative safety of the M200. "You know what to do?"

I nodded. The minute I went through the gate with the crystal, the gate would collapse. Usually there was about two or three seconds of delay, but the collapse would be swift and sudden, and anything caught halfway between the two worlds would be sliced in half. In its early days, Black Division had lost a few soldiers and even some Listeners before they had figured it out. That meant I needed to hang on the back of the APC, drop off before it passed through the gate, and then jump through on foot.

Mendez and I ran back to the APC. The sergeant disappeared inside, and I gripped the ladder on the side of the vehicle, watching for approaching Darksiders. The engine rumbled back to life and the vehicle rolled back towards the gate, picking up speed. I gripped the ladder with one hand, holding the transductor crystal tight against my chest with the other. I felt the wrath and the hatred of the approaching Dark, the whispers of fury growing louder and louder inside of my skull. The hive mind hated us, hated us with an intensity beyond human comprehension, and it was enraged at this intrusion into its world.

That thought pleased me. The Dark had killed billions on Earth. Maybe one day we would have the chance to properly invade their world and repay them in kind.

The gate appeared ahead, and the M200 slowed down.

"All right, Kane," said Mendez over my headset. "Drop down off the back and follow us. Don't dawdle."

"I couldn't agree more, Sergeant," I assured him, and dropped off the side of the M200. I jogged behind the back of the vehicle, and after a moment it disappeared through the gate. Through the hazy ripples and gray light, I saw it rolling onto the deserts of eastern Washington, rejoining the other APCs of our patrol.

With the engine noise gone, I heard the sound, the familiar tearing, metallic whine of an open gate, the same sound I had first heard in Chicago on the night of Invasion Day when all this had begun.

I braced myself for the passage through the gate, my right arm extended behind me, the crystal grasped in my right hand. That way I would have most of my body through the gate before it collapsed.

I glanced back one more time, and I saw a horde of Darksiders moving rapidly through the forest of twisted mushrooms, hundreds of scouts and hundreds of assault drones led by Overseers. I even saw a half-dozen siege drones, huge things the size of city buses that looked like giant centipedes, but much faster than any bus. I felt their alien rage and hate, and something that might have even been fear as they responded to the alien incursion.

Then I hopped backward through the gate.

I left the alien realm behind and landed back in the deserts of eastern Washington. The gate shimmered and shuddered behind me, then snapped out of existence. It was simply gone. There was no trace that a gate had been there at all, save for a line it had left in the sand.

Captain Howard walked towards me, and I nodded.

"You've got the crystal?" he said.

"Yes, sir," I said, holding it up.

Howard nodded. "Bravo Zulu, Kane. We'll take that bad boy directly back to Castle Base."

I let out a long breath, wiping the sweat from my forehead with my free hand.

"That was a cakewalk, sir," Mendez said unexpectedly.

I looked at the devastation surrounding us, the blasted chunks of Darkside chitin, the expended brass shells, and blinked in surprise, half-expecting Howard to rebuke the sergeant.

"Just a walk in the park, Sergeant."

That was my first official combat mission.

Chapter 7

Spokane

Combat missions occupied my life for the next thirteen months.

General Culver had a major campaign in mind. All the gates east of the Cascades and the Sierra Nevada mountains had been cleared by the combined forces of Black Division and the Global Defense Committee, save for the one in Spokane. Intelligence reported that the GDC still had its hands full with the big Darkside strongholds in Los Angeles and Las Vegas, which meant that the Committee didn't have the manpower to make any trouble for Black Division.

That, in turn, meant the General wanted to take out the Spokane gate before turning his attention to the remaining Darkside gates on the Pacific coast.

And before the GDC was free to start looking north again.

Of the various organizations and warlords that had taken control of the pieces of the U.S. after in Invasion Day, Black Division was the most powerful, but the Committee was definitely second. No one else came close, and the United States east of the Mississippi was divided up into various warring fiefdoms that the Dark was overwhelming one by one. Either Black Division or the GDC would have to take charge of the national situation sooner or later, so everyone knew we were going to have to confront the Committee eventually.

But that confrontation would not come until we dealt with Spokane and the GDC dealt with Los Angeles and Las Vegas. General Culver had worked out an informal truce with the members of the Committee that they would hold to a tacit non-aggression pact until the three major western strongholds had been defeated. I didn't know how long the truce would hold, but so far both sides had kept their word, probably because if the GDC diverted any forces from its sieges of Los Angeles and Las Vegas, they would get steamrolled by the Dark.

And the Division would risk the same thing if we turned our attention away from Spokane.

I don't know why Spokane, of all places, became such a major Darkside stronghold. Maybe a really big gate just happened to open there, or maybe the hive mind chose it for reasons of incomprehensible alien logic. Whatever its reasons, the Dark had dug in there in a big way. Their organic technology extended to the creation of buildings as well, and it had grown itself a fortified base there, complete with plasma weapons that served as both anti-aircraft and field artillery. In my first year with Black Division, three major assault forces erupted from the Spokane gate and drove hard for Castle Base; they were only defeated by the general's superior tactics and full support from the Division's limited air force.

One way or another, Black Division simply had to take Spokane and shut down the gate there. Every operation focused on Spokane, and the General gradually constructed a ring of steel around the ruined city, keeping the Dark from breaking out, and destroying any assault forces that tried to break free.

It was inevitable, but our casualties began to mount up over time.

Of the Listeners who had been in my training squad, Nguyen Tran Tong was the first to get killed. We were on the same mission, helping to coordinate a raid on the western edges of Spokane near the line of the old I-90 freeway. Tran was on the northern side of the freeway, helping to coordinate artillery strikes on a fortified enemy position. Either the Dark realized he was there, or they got lucky, because a volley of plasma bolts hit his APC and took him out instantly.

Major Randolph would have chewed Tran's CO a new one for getting a Listener killed, but he got off easy by managing to die in the same explosion.

Later, Major Randolph and the other senior Listeners held a short ceremony for Tran at our forward operating base. I was there, and so were Bull and Jack, who had made sergeant, and Rigger. I was a little alarmed to see how few Listeners there were. The process that made us was unreliable at best. Black Division had captured a few zombies and kept them in secure containment in case someone wanted to volunteer to become a Listener. Of course, with a fifty percent failure rate ending in death, it wasn't surprising that so few people volunteered.

Because the Division didn't have enough Listeners, I went on a mission almost every day. Sometimes it was a patrol in force, like my first mission with Captain Howard and Sergeant Mendez. Sometimes it was an attack, where I was usually involved in spotting for the artillery. A few times, I even rode in a helicopter and helped call in strikes from above. That didn't happen too often, though, because the Dark was good at taking down aircraft. They could use their flying drones as kamikazes, and one scout drone through the engine of an F-16 turned an eighteen million dollar warplane into an expanding pile of scrap. Their anti-aircraft capabilities left Black Division critically short of both aircraft and flight-capable drones.

But the campaign continued, and every week our forward operating bases pushed a little closer to Spokane. Within ten months, our artillery was able to target the Dark's fortifications outside the city. As we took down their strong points, one by one, we moved our forces into the smoking rubble of Spokane's suburbs, setting our own forward bases there. Sometimes the fighting was brutal, block to block and street to street and shop to shop, but the Division's iron ring gradually closed around the gate.

At last, just thirteen months after my first combat mission, General Culver decided it was time for Operation Mousepad.

Yes, that was its codename. Operation Mousepad.

The U.S. military had been prone to giving its operations big scary names in the years leading up to Invasion Day, names like Operation Rolling Thunderbolt of God's Hammer and Operation Giant Fist of Vengeance, and General Culver thought they were ridiculous. Rumor had it that he picked code names by looking around his office and settling upon the first piece of equipment he saw, which might explain why some of the offenses that led up to Operation Mousepad had been named Operation Stapler and Operation Printer.

The name might sound innocuous, but Operation Mousepad promised to be a real doozy.

The Listeners all got a special briefing on the plan.

"Gentlemen," said Major Randolph once we had gathered for the briefing in one of the prefab buildings outside Spokane. "Let's get right to the point. We are preparing for the final assault on the Darksiders' stronghold and gate in Spokane.

This is the last significant gate in the territory that the Division currently controls, and is one of the last remaining major gates between the western mountains and the Mississippi River." He didn't mention the Las Vegas and the Los Angeles gates, probably because they were, at least at present, the GDC's problem. "I do not need to tell you that if we can shut down this gate, it will be a major turning point in our war to liberate America. A victory here would give us the strategic advantage, and free up vital resources for new actions elsewhere. A defeat will cost us dearly, and give the Dark a chance to catch its breath, maybe even open another major gate somewhere in our territory. Therefore, we cannot, and will not, fail."

Jack and Bull and some of the other Listeners cheered. Rigger only scowled, but he always scowled, so that didn't mean anything. I didn't do anything. My natural cynicism, combined with more than a year of experience in the Division, told me that this was going to be a nasty fight.

"We have solid intelligence that tomorrow our rivals to the south," by which he meant the GDC, "are launching a major assault on the Dark's stronghold in Las Vegas. The General and the other senior officers have therefore decided this is an excellent time to finish off the Dark in Spokane. We suspect the hive mind can only divide its attention in so many directions at once, so hitting it with two major assaults simultaneously will increase our chance of success."

"We really want to help those GDC dogs, sir?" said Rigger. For some reason, he really hated the GDC. Sure, he hated everyone, but he especially hated the Committee. Jack's theory was that Rigger had a personal vendetta against someone in one of the cartels that had been absorbed into the GDC. I suppose it was possible.

"The Dark are the enemy, corporal," said Randolph. "First and foremost, our mission is to defeat them. The GDC are merely our opponents. We humans can get back to settling our differences once we've kicked the Dark off our planet and back to their Hell-world." Rigger scowled, but he didn't say anything else, and Major Randolph went back to his briefing.

He had a PowerPoint, of course.

The plan was simple, despite the size of the operation. The Dark's last gate was set in the fortified ruins of the old Spokane Convention Center downtown. Starting at 0600 tomorrow, our artillery would start hammering the fortifications. The armored troops would form spearheads and engage the enemy in the streets, while teams of infantry seized nearby high points and used them to shoot down any flyers. While all this was going on, three assault teams would cross the Spokane River on rafts and rush the gate while the rest of the attack held the attention of the enemy.

"Each assault team will contain two Listeners," said Randolph, much to our surprise.

I blinked. Listeners seldom made direct contact with the enemy, much less joined assault teams. We were too valuable and too difficult to replace. Granted, I had been in a lot of firefights in the last year, but usually from the safety of an armored vehicle or an overwatch position. Still, I think this was the first time the operational plan had involved sending Listeners to the front. And the fact that redundancy was required made it pretty clear that the General didn't expect all of us to survive the attack.

"You may be wondering why the plan includes a break from our usual tactical doctrine," said Randolph. "We think the Spokane gate is powered by a unique transductor crystal, which explains its unusual resiliency and size. Based on the scientists' calculations, anyone but a Listener who handles the transductor crystal for the Spokane gate will either be instantly killed or go insane."

Silence answered that cheerful announcement. That was why they needed two per team. Just in case one didn't make it to the gate.

"Do we have any idea of what the terrain is like on the other side of the gate?" said another of the Listeners, a man with a captain's rank.

"We do not," said Randolph. "However, we know the crystal will have to be within one kilometer of the gate. The scientists have decided that it is mathematically impossible for a transductor crystal to be any further in than one kilometer from an open gate." That matched up with what I had seen in the field. I think the deepest in I had ever gone to retrieve a transductor crystal was only five or six hundred meters. "Additionally, reinforcements have been coming through the gate on a five day cycle. Those reinforcements are coming through right now, which means we'll have to fight them here on Earth. If all goes well, the area of the Dark's world inside the gate ought to be relatively clear. The transductor crystal will probably be a little larger than usual. As usual, once we enter the gate, we will seize the crystal and immediately withdraw back to Earth. Are there any questions?"

There were more than a few, and I listened as the other Listeners asked the major about various aspects of the operation. It seemed tough, but doable. It wasn't going to be an easy fight, by any stretch of the imagination, but I had enough military experience by now to recognize that we had the necessary firepower to make it work. The problem was that we were going to take a lot of casualties. I hoped I would not be one of them.

That night I made sure to call my sister. Maggie was doing well. Frankly, I think she was doing better at Castle Base than she would have under Dad's guidance. Dad had prepared us well for a world at war with the Dark, but I don't think Maggie would have grown up the way she did at Castle Base, because Dad would never have let her become so popular, and everyone loved her at Castle Base. The Division was short of good IT people, and Maggie was tireless when it came to thankless data entry. So she was alternating her time between going to the base's school and working in the IT offices.

She was healthy and happy. I hoped she would be able to stay that way.

And to make sure of that, the first step was to close the Spokane gate.

Right at 0600, the artillery bombardment began.

I waited with my team on the northern bank of the Spokane River, across from the old convention center. The Dark's invasion and the subsequent war had shattered the city, its streets now paved with rubble, and entire neighborhoods were burned-out shells. Yet the empty shells of the old downtown buildings jutted into the sky across the river, and the Darksider citadel squatted in the midst of them.

It looked sort of like a giant turtle, albeit a giant turtle with black spikes jutting from its shell. The spikes weren't decorative. They were the emitters for a plasma weapon like those the Overseers carried, and they could shoot down helicopters with ease. They could also bombard other neighborhoods of the city, but they had trouble hitting anything on the ground within a few hundred meters of the citadel's base. Still, if the Dark saw our assault teams coming, they would have no trouble whatsoever blasting our boats out of the water.

I was in a platoon of twenty men led by Captain Howard and Sergeant Mendez. I was glad that they were in charge of the platoon, since both of them knew their business and had steady heads. Bull and I were the Listeners assigned to them. As the other men checked and double-checked their weapons, Bull and I did a last check of our own equipment, though Bull was praying in silence the entire time. I knew him well enough to know what he was doing, since his lips never stopped moving in silence when we were heading into danger.

I hoped that God was listening. Even after a year of war, I was still a bit shaky on God. I figured He probably existed, but that He hated us. He must, to let the Dark come through their Hellgates.

But maybe He hated them more. I don't know. I just hoped He was listening to Bull. I finished up my check as Bull wrapped his up, his mouth still moving in silent prayer.

Then the clock hit 0600.

The explosions rang across the river, and I saw the bright flare of high explosives striking near the massive citadel. There were more explosions across Spokane, and the spines covering the citadel began to glow as they gathered energy for a plasma discharge. Fortunately, the artillery began to hit home, and the explosions began shattering off the spines. The barrage took off about half of the plasma emitters, mostly those closer to the ground. The citadel could still shoot down any aircraft, but hopefully it would not be able to direct any fire towards the ground.

We waited, listening to the roll of explosions. I glimpsed hordes of Darksiders pouring out from the citadel, rushing to meet the Division's offensive on the other side of the city. Another volley of explosions shook the citadel, snapping off more of the spines. Most of the Darksiders moving out from the citadel looked like assault drones, and in the cramped confines of the city streets they would be absolutely brutal.

The radio headset inside my helmet crackled.

"Strike Teams Alpha, Bravo, Charlie, Delta," said General Culver. "You are go. I repeat, you are go. And God go with you."

"You heard the General," said Major Randolph, who was in charge of the amphibious assault. "All teams, get to your rafts and go. Meet you at the gate."

We hurried down to the river bank where our rafts awaited. Each team had two inflatable rubber rafts with an outboard motor attached. I got on one raft with Sergeant Mendez and ten men, and Bull got on the other raft with Captain Howard and ten other men. The idea was that if one raft sunk, the team wouldn't lose both of its Listeners.

A moment later the engines started, and the rafts began sliding across the waters. The Spokane River has a lot of falls and rapids, but we were upstream from them, and the rafts got us across without incident. I breathed a sigh of relief when we hit the other side. It had been the river crossing, without any cover, that scared me most. Once we reached the opposite bank, we dragged the rafts up after us. No telling if we might need them for a quick escape.

The rumble of constant explosions and the crack of gunfire from the rest of the city had gotten much louder. Operation Mousepad was in full swing. If we were going to close the gate, this was our best chance.

"Move out!" said Howard. Sergeant Mendez gave a stream of orders, directing men to their position in the column. Bull and I went in the middle. That way we wouldn't walk into any traps the enemy had set, and if they came at us from behind, we wouldn't be the first targets in any attack from the back.

We jogged quickly towards the black dome of the Darkside citadel, each team moving off on its own predetermined course. We zigged and zagged past the ruined high rises that had once held shops and offices and condos, past the burned-out hulks of wrecked cars that littered the debris-choked streets. It was hard to believe that this place had once been a city of two hundred thousand people. Now it was just a rubble-strewn graveyard. It looked like something out of a post-apocalyptic movie.

Except we were now living the apocalypse.

"Hold up," snapped Mendez. "Delta group's encountering resistance." He spoke a series of orders into his microphone, listened, and then nodded. "Sir, suggest we circle around the back of the block. The street ahead is blockaded, and Delta and Charlie groups are trying to fight their way through. They ran into assault drones and three Overseers with plasma guns."

Howard nodded. "Fine. Let's move." I almost protested that we ought to go help the other teams, but I knew better. The mission was to close the gate. It didn't matter how many Darksiders we killed today if we didn't close that gate. The Dark would just send more.

We jogged through an alley between the damaged shells of two high-rise buildings. Debris and chunks of twisted steel I-beams littered the alley, and I was careful not to trip. It would be just too stupid to break my ankle right in the middle of a vital mission.

A few moments later we emerged from the alley and were at the base of the citadel, which loomed over us like some huge alien creature. Which, since it was organic, I supposed it was. It was hot near the thing, partly from the waste heat from the plasma discharges, and partly from the metabolic heat the huge building gave off all on its own.

"Entrance is ninety meters that way," said Mendez, pointing at an opening in the base of the citadel.

"Right," said Howard. "Let's–"

It was right about then that something went badly wrong.

That's the thing about war. No matter how carefully you plan, no matter how thoroughly you train, no matter how completely you prepare, something that no one expected always goes wrong.

And when it does, good men die.

One of the damaged plasma emitters high on the dome apparently tried to fire at a target on the other side of the city. From what I understand, the Dark's plasma weapons work by wrapping a magnetic envelope around some superheated plasma, and then shooting it towards the target. Except this plasma emitter had been chewed up by artillery shrapnel, so it wasn't able to generate a proper magnetic bottle.

Which meant that the emitter blew up, and sent out five or six wild streams of plasma in different directions, one of which hit the street right in front of us.

There was an explosion, asphalt fountained into the air as if it was water, and everything went white.

I flew up into the air and hit the wall of the building behind me, my helmet bouncing off the wall, then I struck the sidewalk. The plasma stream had been diffused, at something only like a third of its proper strength, which was the only reason

I wasn't incinerated. For a while I wasn't coherent, and then the smell of burning Kevlar and meat brought me back to cold, harsh reality.

There was a big smoking hole in the street, and the platoon was gone.

All of them. All of them were just dead. Those nearest to the impact point were nothing more than twisted, charred husks. The men further away had been killed by shards of molten stone that had pierced vital organs. I spotted Howard and Mendez, both of them dead. They had been killed so fast they probably hadn't known what hit them.

Bull lay a few feet away, a chunk of cooling stone jutting from his chest.

"Bull?" I said, and I felt stupid. He was obviously dead. At least it had been quick. A wave of emotion rolled through me, so strong I couldn't identify it. Rage? Yeah, there was a lot of that. Grief? He had been my friend, and a good man.

"I hope you like Jesus when you meet him," I told his corpse.

Then I heard a clicking noise, and that jerked me out of my stupor.

A trio of hunter drones were moving down the street towards me, big, ugly things that looked like human-sized mantises, albeit with scorpion tails that fired volleys of poisoned spines. Reflex and training took over, and I snapped my M4 up and started shooting. My first two shots took a hunter drone through the head, and the other two fired spines at me. I ducked, and the spines bounced off the ground.

I came back up, flipping the gun to full auto, and put one burst through the first hunter drone, and another burst through the second. The spines were coated with a neurotoxin, but a gun could fire far more quickly than the launcher in the tails of the hunter drones.

I kept my gun leveled at them, but they didn't move.

Right. I had to keep moving. Someone had to get that transductor crystal, and it might as well be me. I tapped my radio, trying to report in my location and get an update on the status of the battle, but I only heard static. The shock wave from the explosion must have damaged my radio.

Or maybe the Dark had wiped out the other assault teams too, and I was the only one left.

I jogged down the street, heading towards the gaping black hole of the citadel's entrance. Nothing else moved on the street, though the roar of explosions and the chatter of distant gunfire was a constant background noise. I ran faster, trying to get to the entrance to the citadel before anything stopped.

Two assault drones burst from the entrance, their legs clicking against the ground. I cursed, took aim, and started shooting. I sent bullets into the first drone, aiming for its head, and I managed to penetrate its carapace and hit its brain. The creature went into a jerking dance and collapsed to the ground, black slime leaking from the gunshot wounds. The second assault drone was heading right for me, and my M4 clicked empty. I jettisoned the empty clip and jammed a second one into the weapon, but I wasn't fast enough. I would have time to get off a couple of shots before the assault drone ran me down, but that wouldn't be enough to kill the thing.

Then I heard the roar of nearby gunfire, and someone started pouring bullets into the assault drone. I finished reloading my own weapon and joined my fire to the attack, and the assault drone staggered, went limp, and collapsed to the street.

I looked up as two men in fatigues and body armor identical to my own jogged towards me.

"Roland, you all right?" said one.

My brain, still a little woozy from the explosion, snapped back into focus. It was Jack and Rigger. Both were dusty and a bit battered-looking, but as far as I could tell, they were uninjured.

"Yeah," I said. "Yeah. My team's not, though. There was a rogue plasma discharge from the dome. Took them all out. I was right at the edge of the explosion, but everyone else is dead."

Rigger swore several times.

"I've seen it happen before," said Jack. He glared up at the dome. "Those spines leak plasma if they're damaged and they try to fire, I guess they blow up. Charlie and Delta are pinned down. I think we're the only ones who made it this close to the entrance."

"Where is the rest of Bravo?"

"Don't know. We got separated."

"What are we going to do, Sergeant?" I said. Jack outranked both Rigger and me, so he would have to make the call.

"We keep going," said Jack without hesitation. "We fulfill the mission. If we don't get that gate closed, a lot of men will have died for nothing."

"Won't bring them back," grumbled Rigger, but he didn't complain further as he checked his gun.

"Let's go," said Jack. "I'll take point. You two watch my back. Try not to shoot me in the back."

Rigger snorted. "If I'm going to shoot you, Sergeant Walter, it'll be right between the eyes."

"Just shut up and follow me," said Jack.

Rigger offered no complaints as he took the left behind Jack and I took the right. We jogged around the base of the citadel, its dark mass rising over us, and came to the entrance. I expected to see a mob of drones charging out to fight us, but nothing moved in the gloom beyond. Evidently every Darksider in the city was already engaged with the enemy, and no reinforcements had come through the gate yet.

Walking through the entrance was disturbingly like walking through the mouth of some giant creature, an impression reinforced by the organic appearance of the chamber beyond. It was roundish, with glossy black floors and ceilings and walls, and red veins pulsed and throbbed on the walls, giving off a sickly red light. The smell… there weren't words for the smell. It was an alien reek, a weird mixture of the dusty smell of a spider's web and the fetid stink of a swamp under the noon sun.

There was another archway in the distance, and through it I glimpsed the pale familiar light of an open gate.

"Gate's that way," said Jack.

"Of course it is," said Rigger. "We can all sense it." Jack looked at him. "Sir."

"Either of you sense anything?" said Jack.

"Yeah," I said. "But not in here with us." I could sense the throbbing pressure of the gate and the transductor crystal, hear the whispering hisses of the communicating Darksiders, and feel them moving around outside the citadel, but I didn't think there were any in here with us.

That wasn't going to last.

"All right, let's hurry up," said Jack, and he jogged forward, Rigger and I following him.

We entered a vast chamber, easily half the size of the entire citadel. Veins as thick as a grown man covered the walls, glowing with sullen light, and I saw thousands of bundles of things that looked like purple fiber-optic cables bound to the wall, glowing and dripping with a foul-smelling slime. The floor was a bit soft, like a safety mat, and gave off an unpleasant squishing sound with very footstep.

The gate yawned open before us.

It was the biggest gate I had ever seen, big enough that an F-16 fighter jet could have rolled through it without much trouble. Beyond I glimpsed the nightmare world of the Dark, and the whining metallic sound buzzed in my ears. I could neither see nor sense any Darksiders in the chamber, and I couldn't sense any of them beyond the gate.

That didn't mean anything. The senses of a Listener did not always function properly when trying to reach through a gate.

"Through the gate," said Jack. "Follow me."

Rigger and I followed him through the gate and into the world of the Dark.

It was just as I remembered it from previous visits. We were on a plain of black grass-like plants, one of those forests of giant black mushrooms about a kilometer away. The sky was still the color of blood, twisting black clouds flying overhead far faster than the wind would have indicated. Behind the forest I saw a row of mountains, and to my right, a few kilometers away, was a city of giant obsidian structures, like the citadel back in Spokane but far larger.

The transductor crystal was only about three hundred meters away.

It floated above the corpse-flower-like plant, its surface pulsing and flickering with glimmers of white light. The thing was about the usual size, about the width of a volleyball, but it looked more complicated. I realized that it had more facets than the normal crystals. The most facets I had ever seen on a transductor crystal had been ninety-six, but I was willing to bet this one had at least twice as many more.

And I felt different in my head. Usually the crystals had a feeling of pressure, of sharpness, but this was accompanied by a weird buzzing noise I could only hear inside of my head. It sounded almost like a TV show playing through a really bad speaker.

It almost sounded like the crystal was trying to talk to me.

"You guys hear that?" said Rigger, unease going over his ugly face.

"Yeah," I said. "Guess Major Randolph was right. This one is special."

"Special or not, it's coming back with us," said Jack.

We headed towards the crystal. It floated over the flower-like thing, seeming to bob gently as it revolved.

"Rigger, you carry it," said Jack. "Kane and I will cover you."

Rigger grunted. "Right, I… look out!"

We all felt it at the same time, and we looked towards the sky simultaneously.

I had never seen a flying assault drone before. The assault drones were big, so big that I doubted they could fly, but the creature diving towards us had massive blurring wings the size of a basketball court. The bulk of the drone in the center almost seemed like an afterthought. The huge wings folded up as it landed, and Jack, Rigger, and I all tried to scatter.

Jack and Rigger dodged.

I didn't quite make it.

Something stabbed through my stomach and burst out my back, and my left leg exploded with pain. I would have screamed, but I was in too much pain to manage it.

Also, I was flying. The impact had thrown me into the air.

I hit the ground hard at the base of the corpse flower-thing and heard something crunch inside me.

I blacked out for a little bit.

When I woke up I was in a lot of pain, and Jack and Rigger had killed the assault drone. They were standing over me. Jack was frowning. Rigger was scowling. I looked down at myself. There was a lot of blood on my stomach and more on my left leg, and everything below the level of my chest just hurt. I also felt light-headed and a little detached from the pain, which wasn't good.

I wondered if my father had felt this way right before he died.

"He's done for," said Rigger.

"He's still alive," said Jack.

"Yeah, but not for long," said Rigger. "Look, we ought to put a bullet in his head and go. We've got to get the crystal and get out of here. We stay here, the Dark will eat us. And we can't leave Kane here alive for them."

"I'm not leaving a soldier behind," snapped Jack.

"Rigger's right," I rasped. Was that my father speaking or me? "I'll just slow you down. Just give me my gun, I won't let them take me alive."

"Look, Sergeant," said Rigger, ignoring me. "You don't want to do it. I can do it."

"No, there's another way," said Jack. "Roland can carry the crystal, and we'll carry him." He looked at me. "Can you hold onto it?"

"I..." I wanted to tell him to have Rigger shoot me and leave before it was too late. But something inside me rejected the thought. If the Dark wanted my life, they would have to come and get it. I wasn't going to do their work for them, and I wasn't going to let Rigger do it either.

And I was the only family Maggie had left. I couldn't die and leave her alone in the world.

"Yeah," I said. "Give me the crystal and I'll carry it. But if I drop it, take the crystal, shoot me, and run. Don't get yourselves killed on my account."

Jack nodded and stepped out of my field of vision. A few seconds later I heard him swear, and I felt the shift in my mind as the transductor crystal moved.

"That feels... weird," said Jack. He came back into sight, holding the transductor crystal. "Here. Watch out."

He lowered the crystal, and I forced my arms to move through the pain and grasped it.

A strange sensation pulsed through my head.

He was right. It did feel weird. Whenever I held a transductor crystal, my abilities as a Listener seemed to sharpen and come into focus. I heard the communication of the hive mind all around us, and I felt the strange presence of the crystal between my hands. It felt different than the other ones, and I had the distinct feeling that the crystal was trying to tell me something. Maybe that was just the pain and the blood loss.

No. It was something else. It wasn't trying to talk to me.

It wanted me to do something.

It was... was it a user interface? Like a command prompt? I didn't like computers all that much, but Maggie had told me about her database work for the Division. There was something called a command prompt where you could type instructions to the computer. The prompt was the computer prompting you to enter commands, to tell it what to do.

I had the feeling that the presence in my mind was a command prompt of some kind. Like the crystal wanted me to tell it what to do…

Then Rigger grabbed my knees and Jack grabbed me under the arms, and I forgot about the crystal in the wave of pain that roared through me.

"You all right?" said Jack. "Don't drop it!"

"He's gut-stabbed," said Rigger. "Yeah, he's great."

"Go," I croaked, clutching the crystal against my chest as if my life depended on it.

I suppose it did.

Jack and Rigger broke into a shuffling half-run. Every step sent agony through me. You know how you're not supposed to move a severely injured person because you might exacerbate their internal injuries? I can tell you first-hand what great advice that is. Every step jarred me, and I could feel it tearing things inside me. I tasted something metallic in my mouth. Blood, that was it. Maybe the Dark wouldn't kill me. Maybe I would just bleed to death. At this point, that felt almost like a victory.

It was only 300 meters, but it took an agonizing eternity. Or it felt like an eternity. In reality, I don't think it took Jack and Rigger more than two minutes to run from the crystal flower to the gate. I felt every one of those steps, even as I felt the strange presence of the crystal in my thoughts. I also felt thousands of Darksiders rushing towards us in panic. The evil inhabitants of this obsidian Hell city were coming to kill us.

"Sideways," said Jack. "Turn sideways." He was panting. "Both of us go through at the same time. "Else we'll cut him in half when the gate closes."

Rigger said a bad word, but I felt myself rotating with them. To the right, I saw the glow of the gate back to Earth. To the left, I saw the Hell city and the twisted purple jungle, and against the writhing black sky I saw the outline of hundreds of Dark flyers hurtling towards us like attack helicopters.

"Now!" said Jack.

White light filled my vision as we passed through the gate.

Then the gate snapped closed, and we were back in the huge chamber at the heart of the citadel. Both Jack and Rigger stumbled and dropped me, and I hit the ground hard, the crystal rolling off my chest to come to a stop a few yards away against the rubble on the floor.

I was in far too much pain to do anything but lie there, panting in agony.

Fortunately, it didn't take me long to pass out.

Chapter 8

Recovery

I didn't die.

You probably knew that, on account of how I'm still telling this story and all.

I didn't die, but I came close. If I had just been a common infantryman, I probably would have died. My wounds were pretty bad. But I was a Listener. Black Division didn't have nearly enough Listeners, and nearly a third of our Listeners had been killed in the attack. So I got a helicopter ride back to Castle Base and the hospital while other wounded men did not.

It wasn't fair. But life isn't fair, and for once it wasn't fair in my favor, which is why I am still here to tell this story.

I don't remember much of the next three weeks. Only flashes, here and there.

The roar of the chopper's rotors, and the medic shouting something at the pilot.

The lights flashing over the ceiling as I lay on a gurney wheeled along a corridor. Someone was screaming. It was a really annoying sound and I wished the screamer would shut up.

Then I realized it was me. That was embarrassing.

Someone put a mask over my face, and then everything went black.

The next thing I remember clearly is the dream.

I was standing in the Dark's twisted world, in one of those purple jungles of glowing mushroom-things. Maggie stood a few yards away, both hands grasping the complicated transductor crystal I had nearly gotten killed to claim. She was staring into it, both her hands as steady as stone.

Her eyes rose from the crystal and met mine. Her face was blank, utterly free of all emotion.

"You are human," said Maggie. Her voice sounded strange, flat and unemotional, almost like she was reading from a technical manual.

"Yes," I said.

"But you have been altered," said Maggie. "The technology of the weapon has modified your physiology. You can now engage in a limited form of communication with the network."

"Um," I said. "What?" I admit I sometimes didn't know what Maggie was talking about, especially when she got going about SQL databases, but this didn't sound anything like her.

"You are human, but modified," said Maggie. "This may be of use."

"Okay," I said.

"The war is over," said Maggie.

"No, it isn't," I said. "That was just Spokane. There are lots of gates still left."

"Your mode of perception is inadequate," said Maggie. "This method of communication is inefficient. Your cognitive processes require you to consider information through word-symbols, and symbols inherently contain a degree of inaccuracy."

"I don't understand," I said.

"Yes," said Maggie. She looked back into the crystal, lost in thought. "The war is over."

"Considering that I might be dead and in a really weird Hell because of that war," I said, "I think I can safely say that it isn't."

"No," said Maggie. "You are still alive. The war is over. Listen carefully. A long time ago there was a war."

"How long ago?" I said.

"For the purposes of this discussion, the precise timescale is irrelevant," said Maggie. "Your race has not yet devised mathematical-symbols and processes for comprehending time on that scale. Suffice it to say it was long ago. In this war, two powerful races tried to destroy one another. They both succeeded, and both perished in due course. But their creations continue to fight the war, even though it is long finished."

"I don't understand," I said, confused.

"Endeavor to do so," said Maggie. "You do not understand the weapon. But others of your race do, and they will attempt to take control of it. That would be catastrophic. The power of the weapon should not pass into human hands." She shook her head, and for the first time emotion went over her face. It was irritation. "This method of communication is limited, but it is the best you can manage for now. Human biology is not compatible with the weapon even under ideal circumstances, and these are far from optimal circumstances. I can only communicate with those like you, and even then, only with your subconscious mind. Nevertheless, you must remember this."

And then she was gone.

After the dream, or maybe the nightmare, ended, there were more flashes. Hospital beds and doctors and nurses staring down at me. Machines beeping. Tubes in my arms and down my throat.

Maggie sitting in a chair next to a hospital bed, crying.

Then the flashes of memory linked together, and I woke up.

I let out a long, stuttering breath. I felt terrible, with that familiar wooziness that meant I was on painkillers. I was lying in a hospital bed in Castle Base's infirmary. In fact, I think it may have even been the same bed where I had woken up after the zombie had infected me. I blinked my gummy eyes into focus, and saw Maggie sitting next to me, frowning as she typed on a laptop.

Her expression was so like the dream that I was confused for a moment.

"Maggie?" I croaked.

She flinched so violently that the laptop almost fell out of her lap.

"Roland?" she said.

"Yeah," I said. "Guess I'm not dead."

She pushed aside the laptop, grabbed my hand, and started crying, but they were happy tears.

The next few months were unpleasant enough that I wished I could have slept through them, too. Still, it could have been worse, and you can't attend physical therapy when you're unconscious.

Major Randolph visited me first, once Maggie had to go back to work. He filled me in on what had happened after I had passed out in the citadel. Jack and Rigger had managed to keep me from bleeding out, and called for medical evac for me.

"Then we took the city?" I said.

"We did," said Randolph. "It was a hard fight and we lost a lot of good men. Too many. But Spokane is ours, and you and Sergeant Walter and Corporal Rigger closed the gate.

The Committee also managed to shut down the gate at Las Vegas, so the Dark has been cleared from the Cascades to the Mississippi."

"Wow," I said. "That's good news."

"We're already making plans to attack the Dark gate in Seattle," said Randolph. "There's a lot of hard work to do yet, but this was a major victory. Maybe even the turning point. If we can crack the defenses at Seattle, and there is no reason to think that we can't, we should have them on the run."

"Wow," I said again. I was still on a lot of painkillers so it was hard to think of words. "I'm surprised the Dark hasn't struck back."

"They've tried," said Randolph, "but we've been able to detect and close their gates as soon as they open them. Also, the scientists think that the gates draw each other, that it's easier for the Dark to open smaller gates closer to a larger one. With the Spokane gate shut, it's much, much harder for them to open anything in this area, and it's even possible that if they try, the gate might open closer to one of the bigger gates remaining in Seattle and San Francisco."

"Sounds complicated," I said.

"It is," said Major Randolph. "It has something to do with that transductor crystal that you and Walter and Rigger brought back. It's an order of magnitude more complex than the other crystals we've seized, and we think it can somehow control the simpler crystals. We've never seen anything like it before."

"Yeah," I said. "It was weird. I think it was even trying to talk to me in my dreams."

"Was it?" said Randolph.

"I think so," I said. "Or it was just a really weird dream."

"You are on a lot of drugs," Randolph observed. "Rest up, Kane. The intelligence section and the science section both want to debrief you."

"Oh, good," I said. "Any chance I can get a doctor's note and get out of it?"

Both the scientists and the intelligence officers spent a lot of time talking to me, making me repeat my story and over and over until I wanted to hit them, though that would have meant getting out of bed, which wasn't happening. They were particularly interested in the dream—evidently a dream meant more to a Listener than it did to someone without a bunch of Darkside junk in his blood. The overall consensus was that the transductor crystal, which they called a "major transductor crystal", was sentient in some way and had been attempting to communicate with me, though no one could figure out what it had been trying to tell me. The war, after all, was obviously not over. My own theory was that it was just a command prompt, like a computer telling a user to "Press Any Key To Continue", though I had no idea what the crystal's version of a key was.

In between all this, I had a lot of surgery. My left leg had been more or less shattered, and my digestive tract had been badly damaged. In the end, the surgeons reassembled my leg with the help of some space age materials, and I managed to keep most of my intestines. My leg would hurt for the rest of my life, and I would have to be careful about what I ate for a while due to digestive issues, but I would live.

The physical therapy kind of made me wish that I had died. It was almost worse than being wounded.

Jack visited me soon after I woke up, and caught me up on the news. The fall of Spokane was just as big a deal as Major Randolph said it would be, and the morale at Castle Base was way up. The heads of the Mormon Church had even officially declared it proof of God's favor in the war. However, a lot of people thought that the Global Defense Committee might declare war on us now that Las Vegas was out of the way.

"They've got me training some new Listeners," said Jack. "Some of the men who were wounded during Spokane got the conversion weapon into their blood, and we got them back to Castle Base in time for them to undergo the treatment. Some of them actually survived it, so I've been showing them the ropes."

"Sounds boring," I said.

Jack shrugged. "It is. I'd rather be out in the field. Still, no one's shooting plasma bolts at me, so that's good." He grinned. "They're using you as an example, you know."

"What?" I said.

"Of a heroic Listener who did his duty and helped win the battle of Spokane," said Jack.

I groaned. "Great. Just so long as they don't want me to give a speech."

"Don't worry, I don't think anyone is interested in your opinion," said Jack. "Still, I'll bet they will make you take a picture."

To my mild surprise, Rigger visited me as well.

I had fallen asleep, and I woke up to see Rigger standing at the foot of my bed, scowling like he had just taken a bite out of a lemon.

"Rigger," I said.

"Kane," he said. "You look terrible."

"Yeah, well, I'll get better. You'll still be ugly," I said.

Rigger grunted. But he smiled a little.

"You here to finish me off?" I said.

"Nah," said Rigger. "If I wanted you dead, I'd have left you for the Dark." He shook his head. "That was something, you know? What we did. Going in there, just the three of us. That was crazy."

I nodded. "Thanks for not leaving me behind."

Rigger shrugged. "I just didn't want to touch that creepy thing. Walter would have made me carry it."

"Glad I could help," I said. "It was nice of you to offer to shoot me, though."

"Heh," said Rigger. "Figured you didn't want to show up back here with your eyes all black." He looked around. "Hey, you want a drink? One of the guys in Ninth Company's got a still behind one of the supply warehouses. Sergeant doesn't mind so long as we keep it quiet."

"I'm on painkillers," I said. "It'd be a terrible idea. But my liver still works. Give me a shot."

"Good kid," said Rigger. "Just a shot. I'll get in trouble if I get you killed."

"That'd be terrible," I said. Rigger produced a pair of paper cups and a flask, and poured me maybe quarter of an inch of a brown-colored fluid.

He poured himself much more, and passed me the cup. "Here's to your health."

"Here's to not getting gut-stabbed again," I said.

"I'll drink to that," said Rigger, and we both drained our cups.

That stuff burned going down, let me tell you. It was like someone had distilled Dark plasma into liquid form.

"Wow," I said, once I'd stopped coughing.

"Yeah, it's the good stuff," said Rigger. "Rest up, Kane."

He left. And just like that, Rigger and I were solid. More or less. Granted, he was still a psychopath with anger management issues, but he had finally decided we were on the same side. And for my part, I owed him my life. We had done some crazy stuff together, we had survived a horrific experience that was well outside the human norm, and that made us brothers.

Oh well. Like they say, you can choose your friends, but you can't choose your family.

Not long after that, General Culver himself visited me, flanked by a small army of staff officers. Upon review, both the intelligence section and the science section had decided that me, Jack, and Rigger had all performed above and beyond the call of duty, and consequently we got medals. As Jack predicted, they took pictures of us each shaking hands with General Culver as he awarded us the medals, though I had to stay in bed for mine. The General then made a speech praising our efforts in mankind's noble war against the Dark, which was recorded and played for everyone on Castle Base's equivalent of the Internet.

Jack was right. They didn't ask me to make a speech.

Then the physical therapy began.

That really was unpleasant, let me tell you.

Many wounded veterans refer to Physical Therapy as Pain and Torture, and they are not wrong. My leg had been torn up pretty badly, and at first I could barely limp to the bathroom to relieve myself. The torturous regimen of exercises the physical therapist inflicted on me helped with that, and a few weeks later I could mostly walk with a cane, and I was transferred to one of the larger PT classes for soldiers with my kind of injuries.

General Culver joined us for those.

It was his regular practice. He didn't get much time to exercise, but when he did, he came to the PT classes and worked out with the men who had been wounded and maimed under his command. I suppose he felt that he owed us, and I guess he did. I had been hurt pretty bad, but at least my leg was still attached. Some of the other men had suffered far worse. I met men who had lost both legs, or in one case, both hands. One man had taken bad burns to the face. He hadn't lost his eyes, and the surgeons had repaired enough so he could eat and almost talk intelligibly, but his face would always look like a rough mask of reddish scar tissue. I wondered if he would ever find a woman who could look at him without flinching.

But General Culver didn't hesitate to look him in the eye, shake his hand, and thank him for his service. Later, I saw him spotting the guy in the squat rack.

My dad hadn't liked most people, but I could see why he had decided to rejoin Black Division after Invasion Day. The general was a man who could tell you to charge into the gates of Hell, and you would do it without hesitation.

After four and a half months, I was cleared for active duty, and I went back to work. It wasn't like I could really leave Black Division. Despite what the crystal told me in my dreams, there was a war on, and Man was still fighting for his survival. Everyone was needed, even a teenager with a bum leg and a dodgy tummy. I could have taken a desk job helping train new Listeners, but instead, I volunteered to go back into the field. There was so much need for Listeners that I was accepted without hesitation.

I guess I wanted to see this thing through to the end, either the end of the Dark or the end of me, one way or another. I had seen all the carnage and death the Dark had wreaked on us, and I was determined to see them defeated once and for all. This wasn't like any other war in human history. All our other wars had been groups of people fighting different groups of people, and people almost always regret wars like that and wish they could have been avoided. Everyone talks about how things might have been different if someone had shot Hitler or Lenin or whatever, but the war with the Dark wasn't like that. It wanted to annihilate us, and we had to beat it back or be destroyed.

At the time, I thought it was the first war in history where no man was responsible for starting it.

Boy, was I ever wrong about that!

Chapter 9

Rescue

I spent the seven months after my return to active duty going on a lot of patrols in both the Cascade Mountains and the deserts of Arizona.

The major transductor crystal I had taken from Spokane had kept the scientists busy. Jack was better at keeping his ear to the ground than I was, and according to him, the crystal had revolutionized the way the scientists understood the gates. Jack didn't understand the math very well, and I understood it even less, but the scientists thought that the transductor crystals were all networked together, linked in the same way that the Darksiders themselves were linked through their hive mind. The major crystals acted as sort of a combination of anchor and targeting beacon, which was why the Dark found it so much easier to open new gates near a gate that was anchored with a major crystal.

"That makes sense," I said as we sat in the canteen. "Our first year here we spent all that time hunting down scout gates. They would always open up around Spokane. There hasn't been another one since we took the city."

"Yeah," said Jack. "But wouldn't it be great if the scientists were right? Do you realize what that would mean? If we can close all the major gates, the Dark might not be able to find Earth again."

I frowned. "Why not? They got here once, didn't they?"

"Apparently the gates can open anywhere in the universe, right?" said Jack. "And the universe is infinite. If they can't home in on a major gate, then the odds of the Dark being able to find us again are really low."

"How did they get here in the first place?" I said. I vaguely recalled one of our training classes with Major Randolph. "I thought the nuke tests drew them here."

"I wonder," said Jack.

"What?" I said.

"If the nuclear tests drew their attention," said Jack, "why didn't they do anything about it once they got here? There are a bunch of missile silos in North and South Dakota. The Dark controlled most of the area with the silos until the Division got the Dakotas under control, but they never touched the missiles."

"Guess they didn't care," I said.

"Then again, if they didn't care about nukes," said Jack, "how did they come across Earth in the first place? And why at that particular moment in history?"

I snorted. "Cause we're lucky, that's why."

Jack laughed and returned his attention to his food.

But I think the scientists were right about the major transductor crystals acting as anchors. Now that Spokane and Las Vegas were shut down, new gates were only appearing within an observable radius around Seattle, San Francisco, and Los Angeles. That was why I spent so much time in the Cascade Mountains. The Division's next target was going to be the Seattle gate, and we were building a forward position on the west side of the Cascades, getting ready for the final push to the city.

The reason I spent so much time in the desert was the Global Defense Committee.

They were up to something, but the trouble was, no one knew what it was. After they took Las Vegas, the obvious thing for them to do would have been to turn their attention to Los Angeles or San Francisco. Except they weren't doing that. They were probing north, into the territory controlled by the Division, though whenever confronted, they would flee or claim they were only hunting for Darksiders. There were also reports of GDC patrols fighting each other.

The operative theory was that factions within the Committee were starting to fight it out between themselves. It appeared that one faction wanted to go to war with the Division while the other one wanted to leave us alone. Of course, it might have had nothing to do with us. A significant portion of the Committee's armed forces were former footsoldiers for the Mexican cartels, and those cartels had been at war with each other for decades before Invasion Day. Rigger thought that now that some of the pressure was off them thanks to the fall of Las Vegas, they had decided to settle their differences. My idea was that they were just playing a waiting game and had decided to let the Division do the hard work of fighting the Dark. Once we had closed a gate, and paid the price to do so, they would swoop in and grab whatever territory and resources they could while we were regrouping.

As it turned out, none of those ideas were particularly correct.

I found out why when Rigger and I were summoned to a briefing at one of the Division's bases in southern Utah.

"Gentlemen," said Major Randolph when we stepped into the command tent. There were twenty other men in the tent, all of them under the command of a veteran army officer named Captain Ray Vance. Vance and his men had a good reputation as men who got the job done with minimal fuss and casualties, though Vance himself looked more like a beefy construction contractor than a military officer. "Now that we're all here, we can begin. Kane, Rigger, take a seat."

Rigger and I sat on the benches. Major Randolph fired up his beloved PowerPoint projector.

"Before we do start," said Randolph as the projector warmed up, "I will say that absolutely everything you are about to hear is top secret. This isn't to be shared with anyone outside of this tent, understand? Not your families, not your girlfriends, no one." He looked at me. "And not even the other Listeners. Do you understand?"

A chorus of "yes, sir" filled the tent. I was a bit surprised. There wasn't much reason for opsec when dealing with the Dark. It wasn't like they could infiltrate spies among us, and anyone who tried to spy for them would probably get converted into a zombie for his trouble. If this mission required better opsec, that meant we were dealing with human opponents.

In other words, it looked like this mission would have something to do with our friends to the south.

"As you men all know," said Randolph as a map appeared on the screen with the territories controlled by the Division and the Committee mapped out, "recently we have been seeing more and more run-ins with various GDC elements. From what our intelligence agents have been able to learn, it seems some of the founding members of the Committee have fallen out, and they're about to start fighting each other."

Vance grunted. "They do that, they're dead. The Dark'll break out of LA in no time and start ripping them apart."

"I think some of them are aware of that," said Randolph. "Which is the reason we're out here." He tapped his computer, and a new slide appeared, showing a row of headshot photographs. "Thanks to defectors and undercover agents, intel has worked out that there are nineteen senior members of the Global Defense Committee. We've been able to identify eighteen of them." He gestured at the screen. "Most of them are cartel bosses and former Mexican army officers, two are former California state officials, and then there is the one rich guy from Silicon Valley who had the foresight to hire significant private security forces before Invasion Day."

A man with a sergeant's insignia on his fatigues swore.

"What, Hobb?" said Vance.

"I know that guy," said Sergeant Hobb, pointing at the screen. "He's the guy who invented that smartphone game about sheep farming. My ex-wife never stopped playing the stupid thing."

"As Sergeant Hobb just pointed out," said Randolph in a dry voice, "not every member of the Committee possesses meaningful military experience." A low rumble of laughter went through the tent. "Anyway, we've identified all the Committee members except for the nineteenth man, and he seems to be the most important of the lot. He seems to have been the primary brains behind it, and been the key figure in holding these disparate parties together. We believe the reason the GDC has been as successful as it has is because of this man."

"So what's that got to do with us, sir?" said Vance. "The General wants us to kill him?"

"Quite the opposite," said Randolph. "This unknown nineteenth member has requested a meeting with the General, and our job is to escort him out of GDC territory."

Vance blinked, and then said several bad words.

"Our job," said Randolph, "is to meet this man in southern Nevada and escort him to Castle Base for a meeting with the General there. He'll be traveling with a convoy of GDC troops under his command, and we are to meet him here." He tapped a map on the screen, indicating a spot close to Interstate 15 in the southeastern corner of Nevada. "Once we do, we'll escort him to Castle Base for debriefing."

"Sir," I said. "You'll be in command of the mission?"

"That's right," said Randolph. "Captain Vance will be in charge of operations, but final responsibility will rest with me."

"And if both Corporal Rigger and I accompany you, sir," I said, "that's three Listeners on a single mission."

"Yeah," said Vance. "That's a lot of Listeners to lose at once if this goes sour."

Randolph nodded. "It is. My job, and the jobs of Corporal Kane and Corporal Rigger, will be to make sure we avoid contact with any Darksiders. The extraction target indicated that he believes the Dark may be targeting him personally, and requested Listeners to help him escape."

"But the Dark doesn't work that way," said Vance. "They don't target people individually."

"Guy's just paranoid," said Rigger.

"Wait," I said. "But if he requested Listeners, then that means he knows about us and how we work." I looked at Major Randolph. "Should he know that, sir?"

"It's possible," said Randolph. "The Listeners were a secret before Invasion Day, but we've been operating openly since the war started. Thousands of Division soldiers have seen us in action, and word of that has been bound to reach the Committee by now."

"So what if this Committee guy knows about Listeners?" said Vance. "Why send three Listeners to help get him out."

Randolph frowned. "I'm not in the need-to-know loop, but I understand this individual claimed that he has significant intelligence regarding the Dark, and that General Culver found the claim to be credible. That's all I know. And that's all you need to know. Gentlemen, we have our orders and we move out at 0500 tomorrow."

We rolled out before dawn and headed south into the desert.

For the mission, we had six M200 armored personnel carriers, though these had been beefed up with extra armor, guns, and grenade launchers. The Mormons and Black Division had been building factories like mad near Salt Lake City, and they had been churning out fresh armaments. That was good, because I think the Division had mostly burned through its massive stockpile of original armaments, and replacements were needed.

The deserts of southern Nevada were beautiful in an austere sort of way, with lots of scrubland and rocky hills and boulders. When the sun rose to the east and spilled across the land, it looked like someone's desktop wallpaper picture. There wasn't a single cloud in the sky, and soon the temperature began to skyrocket.

The lack of clouds made it easy to spot the plume of smoke from the defector's convoy.

It was about four and a half hours after we had left the base. Randolph, Rigger, and I were each riding in a separate APC, and we all sensed the presence of Darksiders ahead at the same time. About two seconds after that, Sergeant Hobb got on the channel and reported that the men had spotted a big plume of smoke dead ahead.

"Gasoline smoke, sir," said Hobb. "Looks like a bunch of vehicles caught fire right next to each other."

"Like a truck ran into an RPG?" said Vance.

"Yes, sir," said Hobb. "Saw a lot of that in the old days back in Iraq."

Vance used one of his favorite curses. "Major Randolph, how many Darksiders?"

"I'd say nine or ten assault drones heading this way," said Randolph. "Maybe an Overseer. Kane, Rigger?"

"That sounds about right to me, sir," I said, and Rigger concurred.

"Cakewalk," said Vance. "All right, boys, let's greet our unexpected guests."

Vance and Hobb barked orders over the radio channel, and our M200s arranged themselves for battle. About thirty seconds after we were done, ten assault drones raced towards us, dust rising from their legs as they shot across the desert. The gunners and the grenadiers opened up, and the desert bloomed in fire and fountains of dust as bullets ripped into the dirt and grenades exploded. The reputation of Vance and his company was not overstated. Each one of the grenades hit their target and exploded, and the gunners followed up with controlled bursts of automatic fire from the APCs' machine guns. The grenades didn't take the assault drones out, but it did weaken their armor enough to permit the bullets to tear through them.

Vance swore. "One of those drones is going to get through the perimeter."

I was riding in Sergeant Hobb's APC, but through the cameras I saw Vance pop out of the top of his M200, the tube of an AT-4 on his shoulder. A damaged Overseer staggered towards his vehicle, trying to bring its plasma weapon to bear, and Vance fired a HEAT round into it from about fifty meters away.

That took care of the Overseer. Made a mess, though.

"Targets eliminated!" said Hobb.

"Listeners!" said Vance as he dropped back into his APC. "Report! Any more of them out there? Major Randolph?"

"I don't think so, Captain," said Randolph. "Except…"

I frowned. The presence of the Dark had vanished from my senses. I was certain there were no more Darksiders near us.

Except I still sensed something ahead, something I had never encountered before. Randolph was obviously sensing it too.

"Except what? Are all the critters eliminated or not?" snapped Vance. He paused for a half-second. "Sir."

"Maybe," said Randolph. "We got all the drones, but there's something ahead. I don't know what it is. Rigger, Kane? You ever detect anything like this?"

"No, sir," I said. "It kind of feels like an Overseer, but I've never encountered anything like that."

"What he said, sir," grunted Rigger, shaking his head.

"Maybe this defector's got some new kind of Darksider in a cage with him," I said.

"Oh, that's just wonderful," said Vance. "Not only do we have to haul some mysterious Committee defector back to Castle Base, we've got to bring his pet Darksider with him." He said several more words that most officers seldom used in front of us as the APCs continued their advance towards the plume of smoke.

A moment later, the wrecked convoy came into visual range.

It looked like it had been a fierce battle, and there were a lot of dead men and destroyed Darksiders on the ground. Some two dozen wrecked vehicles were scattered amidst the dead, most of them on fire. The wrecked vehicles were a motley assortment of U.S. Army surplus jeeps and Mexican trucks. Looking at the placement of the bodies, it was apparent what had happened. One convoy had been on its way north, and a second group of vehicles had shown up and attacked the first. In the middle of the firefight, the Dark had shown up and killed them all. Then we had arrived, drawn off the surviving Darksiders, and killed them.

It didn't look like anyone had survived.

Yet I still had that weird feeling in my head.

"Orders, sir?" said Vance.

"Bring us to the wrecked vehicles," said Randolph. "Start sweeping the battlefield for any survivors. All the Darksiders are dead, but there might be some GDC survivers. Let them surrender if they can, but if they put up any resistance, shoot them. Corporal Kane, Corporal Rigger, you're with me. We're going to check out this anomaly."

"Sir," said Vance. "The defector. What's he look like?"

"No idea," said Randolph.

"Great," said Vance.

"He did have a code phrase he would use to identify himself," said Randolph. "The phrase is 'for a new global order'."

"Yeah," I muttered. "That's not creepy or anything."

Rigger chuckled at that.

"You heard the major, boys," said Vance. "Get going."

The APCs came to a stop, and we got out. The men went to their positions with professional haste, covering each other with weapons at the ready. I located Rigger and then Major Randolph.

"Wait a minute," said Randolph. "Let Vance's men do their jobs first."

I scowled, but nodded. The cold, cruel logic of the matter was that our deaths would hurt the Division more than the deaths of Vance's men if this went sour, which meant we needed to hang back and let them take the lead. I didn't like it, and it certainly wasn't fair, but wars are not won through fairness.

We waited, the smell of smoke and dead men filling my nostrils, along with the alien reek of dead Darksiders. I started to sweat in the harsh glare of the desert sun. Vance's men moved in orderly groups through the wrecked vehicles, checking for survivors and traps.

"Looks clean so far, sir," came Vance's voice over our radios.

"Very good, Captain," said Randolph. "Kane, Rigger, with me."

We nodded and followed the major. Or, rather, we followed the sense of the strange presence in our heads. We passed the wrecked APCs and came to a truck that was set back from all the others. The hood had been smashed and the engine wrecked by a grenade hit, but the gas tank hadn't ruptured and the vehicle hadn't caught fire. The cab was filled with shrapnel and broken glass, but it looked like the rear of the truck was still intact.

Randolph gestured to us, and I nodded. Rigger would take the right side of the truck, and I would take the left. We would circle around the sides, and then hopefully take off guard whatever was inside.

I circled along the left side of the truck and stopped, my M4 carbine in my hands. After a moment, I glimpsed Rigger and Randolph on the other side, and saw Randolph's fingers ticking down the seconds. Three, two…

One!

I swung around and leveled my carbine at the interior of the truck, Randolph and Rigger following suit. I expected to see everything from a troop of GDC soldiers to a waiting assault drone.

I did not expect to see what was actually inside the truck.

It was empty save for a single army trunk, and sitting atop the trunk was an old man eating an apple.

He was wearing an armored vest, but beneath that, he wore an expensive suit of gray silk with a white shirt and a bright red tie, and even though he was at least eighty years old and he was sitting in a metal box under the desert sun, he wasn't sweating at all. He looked at us with bland interest, and my first thought was that he kind of looked like an emaciated chipmunk. He had deep jowls on his face, but despite that he was lean, almost withered-looking. A shock of hair like snow topped his wrinkled head, and his eyes were a vivid shade of green that looked out of place on that ancient face.

And if my Listener's senses were correct, he was of the Dark.

He felt like… I wasn't sure what it was. One second he felt like an Overseer, and the next it was the same kind of pressure as a transductor crystal. I looked at the ceiling of the truck, half-expecting to see a scout drone hanging up there, but there was nothing. Save for the old man, his trunk, and the apple he was eating, the truck was empty.

I looked at Randolph and Rigger, and saw my confusion shared there.

"Hello," said the old man. "Are you young men from Black Division and General Culver?"

His accent was… odd. His English was perfect, but he didn't always put the emphasis on the right syllable or the right vowel. It gave the impression of a man who had learned to speak English fluently from a book before meeting any actual English speakers.

Something started scratching at the back of my mind. I had seen this man somewhere before, I was sure of it. Was he a Silicon Valley billionaire? He didn't look or sound Mexican.

"Identify yourself," said Randolph.

The old man smiled. "For a new global order."

I looked at Randolph as the old man took another bite of his apple.

"I believe that was the phrase I agreed on with the General during our communications," said the old man.

"Yes," said Randolph.

"Your timing was excellent," said the old man. "Those idiots in the Committee sent their own men to dispose of my escort, which was just as well, since I didn't trust them. Then the Dark fell on us while they fought it out." He sighed. "Ah, isn't that a metaphor for humanity? Fortunately, you finished off the Darksiders before they could get to me."

The sense of familiarity sharpened. I was sure I had seen this man's picture somewhere before, but I couldn't quite place it.

"Those are our orders," said Randolph. "We are to escort you to Castle Base and General Culver."

"Splendid," said the old man. He stood up easily. "All three of you are Listeners? Yes, good. That will make things easier."

"Listeners?" said Randolph. "You know about us?"

"Young man," said the old man, "there are two things in this world I know more about than anyone else. One is the Dark. The other is the Listeners." He considered us for a moment, and then he smiled. It was an unsettling expression. Like his English, his smile was like he was doing an impression of something he had read about and never seen. "Do you know who I am, by the way?"

Randolph gave a slow nod. "Yes."

"Who?" said Rigger, scowling.

"My name," said the old man, "is Mikhail Gregor."

I blinked, and the recollection hit me. Major Randolph had told me that Mikhail Gregor was the man who had invented, or at least funded, the treatment that made the Listeners possible. I also remembered where I had seen his picture before. He had turned up on a lot of the websites my dad had frequented, and those sites had often claimed that Gregor had his hand in every possible international crime since the fall of the Soviet Union, bought and sold national leaders and legislators, and was involved in a plot to inaugurate a tyrannical one-world government.

And he was standing six feet in front of me.

Rigger repeated one of Vance's favorite curses.

"Aptly put," said Gregor. "Will one of you take my trunk? Let's not keep General Culver waiting."

Gregor's presence necessitated a change in our marching order.

The man knew lots and lots of classified information, and Randolph didn't want him sharing it with the rest of Vance's men. So Randolph took over one of the APCs, distributing the soldiers to the other vehicles, and Rigger and I followed him inside. The major drove the vehicle himself, while Rigger and I watched the cameras and kept watch for any enemies. If the Dark attacked us here, we were going to be at a disadvantage.

But I did see the danger of Gregor spilling classified information.

Because that man liked to talk.

I suppose billionaires came to love the sound of their own voices because no one was ever brave enough to tell them to shut up.

Unfortunately, Randolph was busy driving the M200, and Rigger mostly communicated with grunts and profanity, which meant the entirety of Mikhail Gregor's unsettling attention had fallen on me.

"Tell me," said Gregor. "How did you happen to become a Listener, young man? You look barely eighteen, and the Americans always had such scruples about child soldiers, so I assume some sort of traumatic experience was involved."

I hesitated. Randolph had told us to answer questions if asked, but not to speak more than necessary. On the other hand, I didn't feel like spilling my life story to a creepy old billionaire we had found in the desert.

"Hang on," I said. "Information isn't free, you know."

"Ah," said Gregor. A cynical, approving smile went over his withered face.

"But if you want me to answer questions," I said, "it's only fair that you answer some of mine in turn." From the corner of my eye I saw Randolph nod. That was good. He approved of what I was doing. Of course, Gregor saw the nod as well.

"Very well," said Gregor. "This seems a reasonable arrangement. How did someone so young become a Listener?"

"My sister and I were attacked by zombies on the road…" I started.

"Zombies?" said Gregor. "Oh. Yes. The slang for converted human drones. Please continue."

"We were close enough to Castle Base that we made it before I become a zombie," I said. "They asked if I wanted to risk the treatment, and I said yes. I survived it, and that was that."

"Your parents must not have approved," said Gregor.

I shrugged. "The Dark got my dad. My mom… I dunno. They broke up a long time ago and I haven't heard from her in a long time."

"I see," said Gregor. "I can relate. My mother was a harlot."

"I'm sorry?" I said.

"A harlot," said Gregor. He smiled, but the expression had nothing to do with good humor. "Or if you prefer, a whore. I was from a country in the old Eastern Bloc. My mother worked in an establishment that provided the occupying Soviet soldiers with certain comforts. One day a colonel in one of the predecessor agencies to the KGB visited my mother, and I was the result. She usually aborted the unwanted consequences of her profession, but she didn't dare get rid of the colonel's bastard son. So, she got rid of me in a rather different manner as soon as she dared, and eventually my father arranged for me to take a job with the KGB."

"Heartwarming," I said.

"I learned a lot from her," said Gregor. "The strong do as they please, and the weak cope as they can. She hated my father, but because of his power, she had no choice but to submit to his will. Is that not a valuable lesson?" He blinked, and his eyes focused on me again. "Though I am curious. Why were you close enough to Castle Base to receive the treatment?"

"We were going there," I said. "My dad was a soldier in Black Division. A retired soldier, I mean, and he wanted to go to Castle Base to rejoin the Division."

"Ah," said Gregor. "Then your father was a soldier as well? It seems we have much in common, Corporal Kane."

I didn't like that thought at all. "Not really."

"We do now," said Gregor. "I like that thought. Our fathers were on different sides, yes? Had your father in his prime met my father in his prime, they would have killed each other. Now, though, they would have been brothers in our great war against the Dark." That idea seemed to please him. "Tell me, do you have any family left?"

"A sister," I said. I didn't want to tell him about Maggie. Letting this strange old man anywhere near her did not sit well with me.

"I see, I see," said Gregor. "Tell me. You have touched a transductor crystal, yes? When you did, did you suffer dreams afterward where the crystal spoke to you in the guise of a family member?"

He leaned forward a little, his eyes unblinking. He seemed to very much want to know the answer. The intensity of his focus was a little unnerving.

I hesitated. "I think that's classified. You'll have to ask the General about that."

"Ah." Gregor let out a pleased sound and leaned back in his seat. "I see. Yes. I should have known." He smiled to himself. "I should have known indeed. Well, the truth is only obvious in hindsight, is it not?"

"My turn," I said. "I want to ask a question."

Gregor inclined his head.

"Why can we sense you like you're a Darksider?" I said.

"A very good question," said Gregor. "You are aware, I trust, that my scientists developed the procedure for creating the Listeners?"

"Yeah," I said.

"Naturally, I decided to test the procedure on myself," said Gregor. "It worked, but there were certain side effects. I can sense the Dark as you can, but the Darksiders often fail to notice my presence, or perhaps they merely assume that I am one of them. It is occasionally useful."

"You tested the procedure on yourself?" I said. "That's crazy."

Gregor shrugged. "Only if it didn't work. And it did work."

"Why would you do that to yourself?" I said. "I wouldn't have volunteered for this."

Gregor smiled that mechanical smile again. "Do you know why I became a wealthy man, Corporal?"

"For hot women and fast cars," said Rigger. It was the first time he had spoken a complete sentence.

Gregor looked up at him. "An excellent reason, true, but those are only side perks. And at my age, you prefer to drive slowly and take a nap in lieu of feminine company. No, I became a wealthy man because I understand the nature of money."

"A way of keeping score?" I said.

"Another side perk," said Gregor. "No, the nature of money is power, and the core of power is relationships. I didn't become a powerful man because I was rich. No, I became a rich man because I was powerful. Many people do not understand the relationship, but I do."

"Which is why you created the Committee," I said.

Gregor nodded. "A vacuum was there, and I filled it. But before I say anything more, I wish to ask you a question."

"All right," I said.

"Why are you fighting the Dark?"

"That should be obvious," I said. "They're trying to kill me. And everyone."

"Perhaps the question was imprecise," said Gregor. "Why are you here, in the field, and not back at Castle Base? I observed the stiffness in your leg. You must have been severely wounded at some point, and even under the demands of our current war, surely there are rear echelon positions where you could do useful work…"

"Who wants to be a REMF?" grunted Rigger.

"Granted," said Gregor. "But even a committed man cannot remain in the field forever. The spirit may be willing, but the flesh decays. So why are you here?"

I thought over my answer for a moment.

"Because this is important work," I said. "It has to be done, and by accident I have the tools to do it best. So I'm here."

"Because this is a war unlike any other, is it not?" said Gregor. "Every single previous war has featured man warring against man. Not this one. This has united mankind against the Dark."

"Yeah," I said, unsettled. That was near to my thoughts in the hospital bed. "My question. You're Russian, right?"

"Half," said Gregor.

"So what are you doing in the United States?" I said.

"Poor timing, I am afraid," said Gregor. "I was in Los Angeles on Invasion Day. Once I escaped the city with my local bodyguards, I met some other men who shared my concerns over the invasion, and the Committee was born." He shrugged. "I would like to return to Russia one day, but air travel is no longer safe, so that will have to wait. Now I have a question for you."

"Okay," I said.

Gregor leaned forward again. "What kind of crystal was found at the Spokane gate?"

"I think," said Major Randolph from the front of the vehicle, "that this is a conversation that needs to wait until we reach Castle Base."

"Very well," said Gregor, settling back in his seat.

We rode the rest of the way in silence.

We returned to Castle Base about a day and a half later, and at once a troop of soldiers escorted Gregor and Randolph into the command wing. Vance and Hobb were busy seeing to the M200s and their supplies, and I found myself standing alone with Rigger.

Rigger was scowling in the direction that Gregor and Randolph and their escorts had gone. Granted, Rigger usually scowled, but he seemed more annoyed than usual.

"What did you think of Gregor?" I said.

I thought Rigger wasn't going to answer, but at last he spoke. "Reminds me of a guy I knew in prison."

"Yeah?" I said, surprised. Rigger never talked about his past.

"Guy made deals," said Rigger. "He could get you cigarettes or booze or whatever. He also used a lot of pretty words like Gregor there, and he had a nice trick he'd pull. He'd give one gang a set of promises, and then he'd give a different gang the same set of promises. One thing would lead to another, and the gangs would start a riot and wipe each other out. But his hands would be clean, and he'd get all the gangs' stuff. No one ever suspected. But he'd do it again and again." He scowled, and then spat in the dust. "Gregor reminds me of that guy."

"My dad thought he was the antichrist," I said.

Rigger scoffed. "Yeah?"

"Well, not really," I said. "But my dad read a lot of websites where they thought Gregor was secretly plotting to rule the world or was working for the lizard people or something."

"Gregor's been walking around with a bunch of alien stuff in his blood for years," said Rigger. "Maybe your old man's websites were on to something."

That was a disturbing thought. A really disturbing thought. And we had helped bring Gregor to Castle Base.

"That guy you knew in prison," I said. "What happened to him?"

"People got wise to him," said Rigger. "Someone shoved him off a balcony and he cracked his head open on the floor."

I looked at him.

"What?" Rigger glared back. "It wasn't me. I was in my cell at the time. Kind of wish I had done it, though. Guy deserved it."

"Well, don't shoot Gregor," I said. "You'll get court-martialed and shot."

"Nah," said Rigger. "I wouldn't shoot him. That'd be stupid. Have to make it look like an accident."

I blinked, and he grinned and guffawed.

"Let's get some food," I said. "We..."

"Nate! Roland!"

I turned and saw Jack jogging towards us.

"Trouble?" I said.

"Maybe," he said. "We've been summoned to a meeting with the General. All three of us."

Chapter 10

Old Wars

"The Mikhail Gregor?" said Jack as we hurried towards the command wing. "The one who created the Listeners?"

"Yeah," I said. I didn't know if that was classified or not, so I had gone ahead and told Jack what had happened in the desert. He had been as surprised as I had been. Everyone in the Listeners knew about Gregor, since he was the reason that the Listeners existed in the first place. For him to have been the architect behind the GDC was a shock.

"Heck of a coincidence," said Jack.

"It makes sense, doesn't it?" I said. "Explains a lot about the GDC and the way they've been acting. If Gregor built it to fight the Dark and had to recruit help from cartels, bureaucrats, and game developers with money, it explains why all the parts of the Committee are starting to fight each other."

"Wonder why he decided to defect," said Jack.

Rigger grunted. "Bet his friends wised up to him and it got too hot for him."

"And I wonder why the General wants to talk to me," said Jack. "You guys were the ones who found Gregor."

That was a good point, and then I realized the answer.

"Spokane," I said, and the two older men looked at me. "It's because of Spokane. Gregor was asking about it, and the three of us carried the crystal through the gate."

"You carried the crystal," said Jack. "We carried you."

"And you were heavy," said Rigger.

"Well," said Jack, "one way or another, we're about to find out what this is all about."

"Bet it won't be good," said Rigger with dour certainty.

We fell silent as we reached the command wing. Two soldiers met us at the doors and escorted us inside. I had been in the command wing before, and it looked a lot like a typical office building, with desks and printers and filing cabinets. Running an army does take a lot of paperwork, and even though the government had been destroyed, Black Division still needed records and files and all that. The two soldiers led us to an elevator at the end of the hall, unlocked the door, and ushered us inside. While I had been in the command wing before, I had never been in the elevator, and I noticed that the command wing had six levels of basements.

We went down to the lowest basement, and then the elevator continued for one more level after that, a level that didn't show up on the panel.

I had known that Black Division had a lot of secret stuff buried beneath Castle Base, but I hadn't known about this.

The elevator doors hissed open, revealing a long concrete corridor illuminated by harsh lights in steel cages. I took a step out of the elevator and staggered as the sudden presence of the Dark flooded my mind. Had the Division been keeping Darksiders down here? No, that wasn't it…

Jack wobbled a bit and caught his balance.

"You three okay?" said one of our escorts.

"Yeah," said Jack. "Just… caught me off guard."

"Guess we know where they take all those transductor crystals from the gates," I said. I sensed dozens of them around me. I hadn't given it any thought. I knew the science division looked at the crystals, but I hadn't wondered where they did it.

"Sorry about that," said the second escort. "They keep all the weird stuff down here. I guess it's a bit of a shock for you Listener guys. This way."

We walked down the corridor, past reinforced steel doors. I felt the presence of the transductor crystals in my head. They all seemed identical, except for one, a familiar sharp presence that brought a lot of bad memories flooding back.

The major transductor crystal from Spokane was down here, too.

In fact, I thought it was right ahead of me.

And I had the strangest feeling that it could sense me, too.

The corridor ended in a set of reinforced steel doors. One of our escorts stopped, entered a number into a keypad, and spoke what sounded like a code phrase into a speaker. There was an electric buzzing noise, the sound of heavy bolts sliding aside, and the steel doors swung open.

We stepped into what looked like a situation room. A long wooden table ran the length of the concrete room, and a dozen big TVs had been bolted to the wall. The room could have held fifty people, but right now there were only a dozen men at the table. On one side I saw General Culver, Major Randolph, and other high-ranking officers in the Division. Captain Vance was sitting on one end, and he looked a little uncomfortable among so much high-ranking brass.

On the other side of the table sat Mikhail Gregor, still in his gray suit, smiling faintly at the officers of the Division. He looked as calm as he had in that truck, which was strange, because he was sitting in the stronghold of men who were probably his enemies.

In the far wall was a thick window, and on the other side of the window was the major transductor crystal. It had started floating again, and it revolved slowly over a metal table, its black facets flashing with occasional flickers of white light. Suddenly I was back on the other side of the gate, feeling the Darksider's chitin tear into my flesh, and for a moment I was frozen.

The instant after that I had the sudden overwhelming fear that the crystal was about to open a new gate in the middle of Castle Base.

Jack snapped off a crisp salute, and that brought me back to reality. Training took over, and I saluted, as did Rigger.

"At ease, gentlemen," said the General as our escorts left, closing the doors behind them. "Sergeant Walter, Corporal Rigger, Corporal Kane. Thank you for coming. We've asked you here because you were the three Listeners who brought back the object of our discussion." He gestured with a thick hand at the window and the crystal.

"Are you sure you can trust them, General?" said Gregor. His presence seemed to grate against that of the crystal. That faint, humorless smile widened. "The things I am about to share with you are rather dangerous."

Great.

"Every man here has proven himself worthy of trust, often in the most dangerous circumstances," said the General, and despite the strange meeting, I felt a flicker of pride. "Please be seated."

Jack, Rigger, and I sat next to Vance, who nodded at us and then kept glaring at Gregor. It seemed that Gregor also set off the alarm bells in Vance's head.

"Let's begin," said General Culver. "Mr. Gregor, I was not entirely surprised to learn that you were the chief architect of the Committee." Gregor inclined his head in acknowledgment. "But having learned that, I was surprised that you would defect to us. Might I ask why?"

"Because the Committee," said Gregor, "is no longer a fit instrument for my purpose."

"And what is your purpose?" said Major Randolph.

"The complete and total destruction of the Dark," said Gregor. "The experiment, you see, has rather gotten out of hand."

"Experiment?" said the General, his tone hardening.

The two old men looked at each other for a moment. They looked like two old, old enemies getting ready to fight once more.

"You see, General," said Gregor, "I read your PhD dissertation. I read the books of the authors you cited. All the warriors throughout history all say the same thing, do they not? To defeat your foe, you must understand him. Is that not correct?"

"It is," said the General.

"So," said Gregor, "tell me. What is the nature of the Dark?"

"Their nature?" said the General. "This is hardly the time for riddling games."

"It's not a game, General Culver," said Gregor. "It is a deadly serious business, and the fate of the planet and humanity alike depends upon our answer."

The General was silent for a moment. "The best assessment of our scientists is that the Darksiders are a predatory, migratory species, much like a locust swarm. They move from world to world, use up all the available organic resources to propagate themselves, and when they've finished, the open new gates until they find another compatible world and move on to conquer it. We don't know how long they've been doing this or how many worlds they've conquered, but it's probably been a very long time… and Earth is likely the latest in a long line of worlds they've assaulted."

"All that is accurate, General," said Gregor, "but it overlooks one important point."

"Which is?"

"The origins of the Dark," said Gregor. "It did not evolve. God did not create it on the sixth day. Instead, it was engineered."

"Explain," said the General.

"My researchers have made progress decoding some of the information stored in the genetic matrices of the Dark," said Gregor. "And in doing so, we have realized the truth. The Dark was created as a weapon. Long ago, long before human civilization, two great alien races were locked in an eternal war. They were so powerful that to us they would seem like gods, but they were equally matched and so could not overcome the other. Then one of the races engineered a weapon of surpassing power, one that would win the war."

"The Dark," said the General, no expression on his face.

"Precisely," said Gregor.

"How can you possibly know this?" said Randolph. "You dug this information out of dead Darksiders?"

"Exactly, Major Randolph," said Gregor. "Consider your laptop computer. Now consider what would happen if an alien race with no knowledge of humanity came across the device. Just from analyzing it, they could learn a great deal about humanity. From the keys and the screen and the speakers they could make an accurate guess about our physical configuration. And once they taught themselves to read the files on the hard drive, they could learn even more. To extend the metaphor, each individual Darksider is a laptop computer, and they all share a common operating system and firmware. Once we realized that the Darksiders were bioengineered creatures, my scientists were able to learn a great deal from that starting point."

"So what happened to these two alien races of yours?" said the General.

"The weapon was more successful than its creators dreamed," said Gregor. "It destroyed its creators' enemies… and then it turned and destroyed its own creators as well. They had made it too powerful, and the central core that controls the Dark will continue its mission, whatever the cost. The ancient war is over, but the weapon persists, rather like one of those poor Japanese soldiers still fighting World War II in the 1970s. The Dark has been spreading throughout the universe, destroying planet after planet, race after race, and our race is its current target."

It made sense. It also explained a lot of the otherwise inexplicable behavior of the Dark. The Darksiders hadn't adapted very well to fighting us. They were horribly destructive and had killed a lot of people, but they didn't seem to understand fighting humans very well. Most of the Division's oil came from North and South Dakota, and if the Dark had destroyed the facilities there, it could have hindered or even crippled us, but it ignored the refineries and the pumps. It did attack our crops and fields, but that only seemed to be so it could harvest more biomass to build its organic structures, and it was just as likely to strip a forest bare. It had been as if they thought they were fighting someone else.

In hindsight, that was just it. The Dark's inexplicable behavior was because the Darksiders had been designed to fight someone else.

Forget the Japanese guy. It was more like an infected computer that was part of a botnet that kept running its viral program long after its creator had been arrested and put away.

I realized that everyone was staring at me, and then I realized that I had spoken aloud.

"Sorry, sir," I said. "I spoke out of turn."

"No, go on," said General Culver. He was calm, but there was a dangerous glint in his eye as he looked at Gregor. "You were saying something about a computer, Corporal?"

"That's what the Dark is, sir," I said. "If Gregor is right. It's like they're part of a botnet. The hacker was shut down long ago, but his bot is still running, and it won't stop until it's shut down."

"A good metaphor," said Gregor. "Some of the younger scientists tended to think of it in those terms as well."

The General didn't say anything for a while, his fingers drumming against the table.

"You disagree?" said Gregor.

"You knew about this," said the General, "before Invasion Day, didn't you? You didn't find it out in the two years since. That kind of research takes advanced equipment and trained scientists, and there have been shortages of both since the invasion started."

"Of course," said Gregor.

"And you had founded what became the Committee before Invasion Day," said the General. "All that infrastructure didn't spring into place overnight."

A cold, humorless smile spread across Gregor's face. "Once again, yes."

Something happened then that I had never seen before.

General Culver got angry.

He didn't shout, he didn't scream or rave or hit the table, but his nostrils flared and a deep red flush spread from his neck and across his face, almost like a piece of metal starting to glow in the fire. His officers stared at him in astonishment. Gregor only smiled.

"I always suspected," said the General. "I always suspected they would do something like this. The experiment got out of hand, is that what you said?" He leveled a finger at Gregor. "You opened the first gate for the Dark, didn't you? You and your group."

"Yes," said Gregor.

Utter shocked silence hung over the conference room. I stared at Gregor, incredulous, and a tidal wave of rage then erupted through me. I thought of my father, of Maggie sobbing at his grave, of the burning cities and the thousands of corpses I had seen since Invasion Day, of Nguyen Tran Tong's sisters crying when we told them the news, of Bull lying dead in the streets of Spokane. I thought of Rigger and his story about the man from prison.

I looked over at Rigger and saw that his face had gone blank, that he was starting to ease his pistol from his belt.

"Corporal Rigger," said the General, "you will put your weapon away. Now!" He hadn't even looked to the side.

Rigger blinked and slipped his pistol back into its holster.

"However," said the General, still staring at Gregor, "you, Mr. Gregor, are going to explain to me why I should not order Corporal Rigger to shoot you between the eyes right here and now."

Gregor's mirthless smile had never wavered. I don't think I had ever hated anyone as much as I hated Mikhail Gregor in that terrible moment. "I started this war, yes, that is true. That being said, I'm the only one who knows how to end it."

"Explain," said the General.

"You know why I had to do it," said Gregor. "Without a global government to keep its destructive tendencies in check, humanity is doomed. Some like-minded individuals of power and influence have been working with me towards that end. Over the decades we've tried many tactics to move mankind closer to a unified global government—currency manipulation, engineered terrorism and wars, shadow governments, propagandizing via social media, deep states, coups, and so on. However, I am embarrassed to admit that none of them really worked and several of them proved counterproductive."

He leaned forward, his green eyes glittering in that withered face.

"The only thing," said Gregor, "the only thing that has ever convinced mankind to unite has been a common foe. And what better common foe than the Dark? We had already drawn them here by accident. Apparently, some of the radiation from a fission explosion resembles the profile of one of their long-dead enemies. They opened a scout gate or two to investigate, but they otherwise ignored us, since we didn't fit their targeting profiles. That's why the Dark never mounted a full-scale incursion. But my scientists learned how it would be possible to draw a major gate here, and my associates and I settled upon a plan. We would draw a gate here, and permit the Dark to destroy a few cities. It would cost humanity a few hundred million dead or so, a trivial quantity when viewed from the grand historical perspective. Mankind would unite against the alien threat, and a global government would naturally be established to address the danger. Peace on Earth, good will to men, world without end, amen."

"Except the experiment got out of hand," I said, throwing his earlier words back at him.

"Yes," said Gregor, drawing the word out. "It rather did. We didn't anticipate the scale of the Dark's response. I found myself unexpectedly stranded in Los Angeles… and here we are."

"I don't care about your rationalizations," said the General. "I know why you did it. I want to know why you think you can end the war."

Gregor smiled. "With that."

He pointed at the major transductor crystal.

"And just how are you going to use that?" said the General.

"Don't you understand? A major transductor crystal is a living, thinking creation," said Gregor. "It is alive and sapient. It's not life or intelligence as we understand it, but it is alive and intelligent nonetheless. The transductor crystals are alive, and what's more, they're networked together. One can communicate instantly with another, and I know how to talk to the crystals. I know how to tell them to shut down the gates. Permanently."

"If you know how to do this," said the General, "why haven't you done it already?"

"Because I needed a major transductor crystal," said Gregor, "and the ineptitude of my fellow Committee members prevented us from ever capturing one. The major crystals are… how to put this? They possess greater authority than the minor ones. To use Corporal Kane's computer metaphor, the major crystals have greater administrative control and access permissions over the gates. A command sent from a lesser crystal can close a single gate. A command sent from a major crystal can close all the gates at once."

"You had your own little private army as well," said Randolph. "Why didn't you get your own major crystal?"

Gregor sighed. "Competent help is difficult to find, particularly in the midst of an apocalypse. The Committee managed to keep together the motley gang of criminals, brigands, and fools we had assembled long enough to take Las Vegas and close the gate there, but in the process, one of the idiots destroyed the crystal. Naturally, once Las Vegas fell, the infighting and jockeying for position began, and the Committee began to fracture. I realized that if I was to obtain a major crystal and close the gates, I would require more competent help. Hence, my visit here."

"All right," said the General. "You wanted access to a major crystal. There's one right over there. Why don't you go tell it to shut off the gates and end the war?"

"It would be pleasant if life were that simple, would it not?" said Gregor. "Unfortunately, as you have already guessed, the process will be a little more complex."

"Why?" said the General.

"Because humans are not compatible with the biological technology of the Dark," said Gregor. "This is not unknown. The Listeners were supposed to have become converted drones under the control of the central core, after all. Only by altering the invading bio-technology, by 'hacking' it if you will, were the Listeners created. Controlling a crystal works in much the same way. Humans are not properly compatible with the interface, but some degree of control can be exerted through them nevertheless."

"And how does that degree of control need to work?" said the General.

"First," said Gregor, "I need to be in physical contact with the major crystal. Second, I need to be within ten yards of a lesser crystal. Third, the lesser crystal needs to be actively empowering an open gate."

Silence greeted that list of requirements.

"That is indeed a little more complex," said the General.

"We have dozens of lesser crystals here," said Randolph. "Why can't you use one of those?"

"The lesser crystal has to be active," said Gregor.

"Are you seriously suggesting that we open a gate within Castle Base?" said Randolph.

"I would," said Gregor, "but sadly that it is not a viable possibility. I don't know how to reactivate a lesser crystal once it has been shut down. I doubt it is even possible for a human to do so. From what my scientists discovered, only an Overseer or a High Overseer would be able to do so. As I have said, even we modified humans are simply not sufficiently compatible."

"It might be doable to find an active crystal, sir," said one of the other officers I didn't recognize. "There are a number of scout gates in the Cascades. If we took the major crystal to one of them and mounted an incursion, it should be achievable."

"Other than the fact, of course, that Mr. Gregor is not trustworthy," said the General.

"Of course you do not consider me trustworthy," said Gregor. "But, then, you will surely agree that I did just admit to participating in what, from your perspective, must appear to be mass genocide. After that, what further use for deception could I possibly have?"

The General frowned again, tapping his fingers against the table. "And you're the only one who can do it, is that it?"

"I am afraid so," said Gregor. "As you know, I took an experimental version of the Listener treatment before we decided upon the final protocol. I'm afraid it didn't work for me quite the way it did for the others. Your other Listeners have no doubt reported that they can sense me like a Darksider. This means I have a better ability to connect with the intelligence within the major crystal, and the ability to give it limited commands."

"This technique," said the General. "Why don't you teach it to one of my Listeners? You're an old man, Mr. Gregor. Surely you do not want to expose yourself to the rigors of the field."

"Indeed I am an old man," said Gregor, "but I fear it must be me. One, I have a greater connection to the Dark's control core than any other Listener. Two, it took me a great deal of time to learn to communicate with the transductor crystals on any level at all. I might not live long enough to teach the technique." His thin smile returned. "And every moment we delay means that more innocent people fall victim to the Dark. Surely you wish to save as many innocent people as possible, General Culver."

I heard the note of mockery in his voice. So did the others, who shifted angrily in their seats. I don't think there was a man there who would have been unwilling to murder the evil old man.

If he was even still a man. Frankly, I wasn't sure he ever was.

The General remain unruffled. "I also have specialists who might be able to force the knowledge of the technique from you."

"True, true," said Gregor. "Granted, I doubt they are the equal of the specialists I once commanded during my time with the KGB. But I have no doubt of their skill, and I have little enjoyment of pain. But as we have established, I am an old man, and my health is not robust. How long do you think I could bear up under such rigors? My heart might give out in the first five minutes. And then during the long decades of war as you struggle to close the gates one by one, perhaps you will curse yourself for missing the one opportunity you shall have for a quick end to this war."

"I am certain," said the General, "that you are lying to me."

"Obviously I am keeping secrets from you, just as I have always kept secrets from you and anyone else who knows about the existence of the Dark. But every single word I have told to you during this interview has been the truth. I can use the major crystal. I can shut every gate simultaneously. I can end this war in an hour, if you just get me and the major crystal to a functioning gate. Can you really afford to throw away that opportunity, General?"

For a moment, no one said anything.

"Vance," said the General at last. "Kane. Walter. Rigger. Wait outside. We'll call you back in a minute."

I wanted to protest, but I had been in the Division too long to mouth off to the General. I followed the others as we stood up. One of the guards opened the door, and we filed back into the hallway.

We wound up waiting outside the reinforced steel door that led to the room holding the major transductor crystal. I could feel the thing inside my head, its presence sharp and hard. Yet it was also a familiar presence, in the way that the presence of the minor crystals was not. In fact, I was sure that the crystal recognized me. Gregor had said he could talk to the crystal, though it had taken him years to learn how to do it. Could I do the same thing? If I could communicate with the crystal, maybe I could tell it to shut down the gates, and we wouldn't need to rely on a dangerous man like Gregor at all.

I focused on the crystal, trying to do… well, I don't know what? Talk to it inside my head? To my surprise, the sense of the crystal changed a little. It knew I was there. Could I tell it what to do? I focused a little harder, trying to tell it to shut down the gates.

For a moment, just a moment, I thought I saw Maggie standing across the hall from me.

Then the image vanished, and I realized the others were talking. I made myself pay attention.

"This is a terrible idea," said Jack. "We should smoke the bastard. We don't need him."

Vance shrugged. "The General knows what he's doing." He had produced a cigarette from somewhere. I didn't think we were allowed to smoke down here, but the guards didn't seem inclined to stop him.

"Yeah, but that lunatic just admitted he started this war," said Jack. He was pacing back and forth. He only did that when he got really angry. It was just as well that General Culver had ordered Rigger not to shoot Gregor, because Jack might have done it first otherwise. "Everything that has happened has been his fault, and all because he and his rich friends had some crackpot idea about how they should rule the world. The General should have let Rigger shoot him." Rigger nodded his vehement agreement. "Or better, he should have put Gregor on trial. Let everyone know that this was his fault, and then shoot him."

"The General was probably recording that conversation," said Vance.

I blinked. That hadn't occurred to me.

"See, I've been with the Division a long time," said Vance. He snorted. "Probably before some of you children were born. Anyway, the General's just as clever as Gregor. The Division was almost shut down a couple of times in the last ten years before Invasion Day. Usually Congress had a bee in its bonnet about how the General wouldn't accept women for frontline combat troops, though I suppose in hindsight Gregor and his friends might have been bribing Congress to shut down the Division." He shook his head and tapped some ash onto the floor. "The General always outwitted them."

"Do you think Gregor is telling the truth, sir?" I said.

Vance shrugged. "That's above my pay grade. You're the Listeners. You're the ones who can hear the Dark inside your heads. What do you think?"

"I think I want a drink," said Rigger, "right after I shoot that old man."

"I don't know," said Jack. "Roland, what do you think?"

"The major crystal was trying to talk to me," I said, thinking back to the strange dream. "When I was recovering after Spokane, I mean. It appeared as my sister, and it kept telling me that the war was over. I thought it was just a fever dream, but if Gregor's right, if the races that created the Dark wiped each other out... then the crystal was telling the truth. It knows the war that created it is over. Maybe it wants to be shut down."

"Yeah, but Gregor isn't doing this out of the goodness of his heart," said Jack. "What does he want?"

Vance grunted. "Maybe he's had a crisis of conscience. Maybe he's decided to repent, and wants to make up for some of his crimes before he dies."

We all looked at each other, and then burst out laughing.

"Yeah," said Rigger, "that ain't it."

"Didn't think so," said Vance. He dropped the cigarette and ground it out. "But I suspect we're about to find out."

I turned and saw the conference room doors shut, and General Culver stepped towards us. Reflex took over, and I snapped off a salute, the others following suit.

"At ease," said the General. "Men, I'm afraid I'm going to have to give you a dangerous mission."

Vance nodded. "We're going to try Gregor's plan."

"He's lying, sir," said Rigger. I had never seen him look so agitated. "I know a liar when I smell one, and he stinks of it, sir. He's playing us."

"I agree," said the General. "He is a liar, and he is one of the architects of the greatest mass slaughter in human history. But what he told us in there was the truth. He confirmed and indeed proved several of the theories our scientists have held for some time. He was telling the truth, and he's planning to betray us somehow to his own advantage. So we're going to play his game."

"Why, sir?" I said.

"Because he is right about one thing," said the General. "This is our best chance to end the war with a single stroke. Captain Vance, tomorrow at 0500 you and your company will leave Castle Base and head for one of the known scout gates in the western Cascades. Sergeant Walter, Corporal Rigger, and

Corporal Kane, you will accompany Captain Vance's company. Your mission will be to escort Mikhail Gregor and the major transductor crystal to the lesser crystal on the other side of the scout gate, and ensure that he correctly performs the procedure to shut down the gates."

Vance sighed. "You don't give us the easy ones, sir."

"I don't," said the General. "We have other men who can handle the easy ones. When a mission absolutely has to succeed, Ray, I give it to you and your boys."

"Aw, what am I supposed to say to that, sir?" said Vance. He sighed again and saluted. "We'll get it done or die trying. What about Gregor?"

"Your mission is to get him to the minor crystal with the major crystal and ensure that he shuts down the gates," said the General. "If at any point, you suspect he is going to betray you, or if he does anything other than what he promised, shoot him."

"With enthusiasm, sir," said Vance. He looked at us. "All right, men, you heard the General. We've got a mission to plan."

Chapter 11

Interface

At 0500 sharp, we boarded a dozen M200s loaded down with weaponry and rolled out to the west, the Cascade Mountains rising before us.

I rode in Sergeant Hobb's APC with Rigger and Jack, which also meant that Gregor got to ride with us. Gregor, for his part, seemed perfectly calm. He had traded his suit for combat fatigues and body armor, and it seem incongruous to see that withered chipmunk face over that much combat gear. Yet the weight didn't seem to slow him down. If anything, he seemed enthusiastic. Energized, even. There had been a spring in his step as we escorted him from Castle Base and loaded him into the APC.

It was odd to see an eighty-year-old man with that kind of energy. I suppose you don't get to be the kind of billionaire who can buy and sell the souls of politicians without a lot of vigor. Yet it seemed strange, almost unnatural. I wondered if Gregor's Listener treatment had done something to increase his stamina. That didn't seem possible, but it would explain how a man his age had survived the rigors of the last few days without the slightest hint of strain.

Maybe that was one of the things he hadn't mentioned to General Culver.

I wondered what else he hadn't mentioned during our little chat. I remembered Rigger's story and wondered if I shouldn't just shoot Gregor. I know I wasn't the only one. Rigger kept glaring at the old man.

"Why so glum, gentlemen?" said Gregor as our APCs rolled into the desert.

Rigger grunted. "It's early. Haven't had my coffee yet."

Jack snorted and turned his attention to the windows, watching the surrounding landscape for threats. I didn't sense any Darksiders yet, save for whatever was in Gregor's blood and the sharp presence of the major transductor crystal in Vance's APC, but there was always the risk the rest of the Committee had learned of this and might try to assassinate Gregor.

"We are going to make history today," said Gregor. "Another step on mankind's long road to progress. Today we're going to save the world."

"From what you did to it," I said.

"There have been setbacks," said Gregor.

"Setbacks," said Jack, glaring at Gregor for a moment and then turning his attention to the window.

"Setbacks and failures, I admit it freely," said Gregor. "But today I will see the fulfillment of my life's work. How can I find that anything but invigorating?"

"So was your life's work to see Earth get invaded by insane alien weapons?" I said. "If so, good job."

"Ah," said Gregor. "Tell me. Did General Culver order you to kill me once the mission was finished?"

"He did not," said Jack. He had ordered us to kill Gregor at the first sign of treachery, but there was no need to let Gregor know that. Besides, I had no doubt the cunning old man had already figured it out.

Gregor shrugged. "Perhaps he did, and perhaps he did not. But is it not exhilarating? You wait to see if I will betray you. I wait to see if you will betray me. A game with deadly consequences, and the fate of all humanity as the stakes." He smiled that mechanical, humorless smile. "It proves that I was right."

"About what?" I said.

"That the only way humanity will ever unify under one government is in the face of an external threat," said Gregor. "Each one of you would gladly shoot me if given the chance, and if I am to be honest if I were free to act I would liquidate you as potential threats. But here we are, working together for the greater good. There is a valuable lesson in that, is there not?"

"Yeah," said Rigger. "You're a lunatic and you should stop talking."

Gregor's eyes narrowed to green slits at that. I guess he didn't like being called crazy.

"Hey," said Sergeant Hobb from the driver's seat, "you back there, shut up so I can concentrate. I don't care if you're Listeners or billionaires or whatever, but if I drive off a cliff because you're distracting me with your yammering, you'll all die together. So shaddup."

On that cheery note, we stopped talking. At least it shut Gregor up, though the old man still looked enthusiastic. We drove into the western foothills of the Cascades, following the old I-90 line through the mountains. I have to admit it was nice to see green forests again after so much time in the deserts of the western United States. Even after two years of no maintenance, the road was still in decent condition, and we made good time, though the ride was bumpy. Then again, the M200

APCs hadn't been built for comfort. As we descended the far side of the mountains, I felt the distant presence of the major gate in the ruins of Seattle.

And the sharper presence of a scout gate nearby.

"Approaching the town of North Bend," said Vance. "All troops, report in."

North Bend had once been a nice little tourist town surrounded by the green forests of the western Cascades. Now, like so many other little towns, it had been destroyed by the Dark's invasion. Unlike many wrecked towns, it had a scout gate right in the center of town. I felt its sharp presence as we approached the ruins, and also the presence of multiple Darksiders.

"No visuals yet," someone said over the radio.

"That won't last," murmured Gregor.

I glanced at him and spoke up. "Sir, I think there are twenty to thirty scout drones near the gate, and three or four Overseers." Jack and Rigger agreed with my assessment.

"All clustered near the gate?" said Vance.

"Yes, sir," said Jack.

"Right," said Vance. "Well, let's make some noise. Sergeant Hobb, this is what I want done."

The APCs split into three groups. One group would come right down the center of Main Avenue. Two more would come at Main Avenue from either side and hit the Dark from the flanks as they engaged the main group. I watched the street as our APC rolled behind the main force, looking at all the empty houses. I wondered how many people had died here on Invasion Day.

I wondered how many people had died here because of the old man sitting on the bench behind me.

Then the battle began and I didn't have any time to worry about it.

Our APC brought up the back of the main group, and a mob of scout drones flew towards us. The machine gunners opened fire, raking streams of bullets across the drones. They dropped like flies, but they weren't the main threat. The three Overseers behind them with plasma weapons posed the main danger, and we fired a volley of AT-4s at them. That didn't kill them, but it did throw them off-guard long enough for the other two groups of APCs to burst from the side streets and open fire with every weapon at once.

That took care of the Overseers.

"Cease fire!" Vance's voice crackled over the speakers. "All units, cease fire! Get a perimeter around that gate. Move!"

The APCs rolled into position, leveling their weapons at the scout gate. It was about the size of a usual scout gate, maybe ten meters tall and ten wide, just wide enough that one of the APCs could get through it without slicing it in half. With the fluid motions of long experience, the M200 drivers got their vehicles positioned in a perimeter around the gate, machine guns and Javelins leveled at the flickering portal.

"And so it begins at last," murmured Gregor.

I shot him a look, but his withered chipmunk face gave away nothing.

"Listeners," said Vance. "You sense anything on the other side of that gate?"

"Not yet, sir," I said. "But it's…"

"Yeah, yeah, it always doesn't work through the gate," said Vance. "Kane, you drew the lucky straw, so you get to go through the gate first. Sergeant Hobb, assign some men to escort him." Hobb gave the orders, and soon I disembarked from the M200, carbine in hand, and six men came to escort me. They fanned out around me, and we went through the gate as one.

As usual I felt that flicker of strange disorientation, and then I found myself on the Darkside. Or maybe it wasn't really the Dark's world, but the world of their creators, or maybe a world that had once belonged to another race they had destroyed. Anyway, it was the usual black sky with billowing clouds, a distant range of mountains on the horizon. To my left rose one of those mushroom forests, and ahead of the gate stretched a patch of hilly, grassy terrain.

About five hundred yards away I caught the flash of a transductor crystal floating over the corpse-flower plant base.

"Well?" said one of the soldiers. "Any Darksiders nearby?"

"No," I said, concentrating. "Not yet. Some in the mushrooms, and some in the mountains. None of them are here. I think we've got about ten, maybe fifteen minutes before more show up."

"Then let's move," said the soldier, and we retreated through the gate and back to Earth.

"Well?" said Vance once we had emerged. He stood with Sergeant Hobb and ten men, watching the gate with wary eyes.

"No Darksiders around," I reported. "The nearest ones are a minimum of ten minutes away in a forest of the mushroom-things to the left. If we hurry, we can get to the transductor crystal and back before they respond."

"Yeah," said Vance, turning his head. "Course, we're not just trying to close the gate, are we, Mr. Gregor?"

I saw Rigger and Jack approaching, Gregor walking between them. Rigger carried a heavy strong box that contained the major transductor crystal.

"We are not, Captain Vance," said Gregor. "We are attempting to exert total control over the entirety of the gate system."

"How long is that going to take?" said Vance.

"About one to five minutes," said Gregor. "I suggest we hurry. The Dark will have sensed our presence in their world, and they will be hurrying to respond."

Vance nodded. "Fine. Sergeant, half the APCs are coming with us, the other half are remaining here. Once Mr. Gregor has control of the gate network, we'll retreat back through the gate. If he knows what he's talking about, the gates should collapse after Gregor comes through with both the crystals."

"Yes," said Gregor. "I do. If Corporal Rigger could hand over the major crystal now, that would be most helpful."

Vance gave the old man a level stare. "You'll get it when we reach the hill. Back in the APC, Mr. Gregor."

Gregor gave him a thin smile, but followed us back to the APC. Vance joined us, leaving Sergeant Hobb to command the perimeter back on Earth.

"We're ready, sir," said Hobb.

"All right," said Vance, settling himself into the driver's seat. "See you shortly, Sergeant, God willing. Everyone, follow my APC."

He tapped the throttle, and the APC rolled through the gate and into the Dark side.

I flinched as we went through the gate, a new sensation rolling over me. I had never carried a crystal back through the gate, and it felt strange. I could also sense Gregor. I mean, I had sensed him during the entire journey from Castle Base, but now his presence felt sharper, stronger.

He felt…

He almost felt like a walking major crystal.

I shared a look with Rigger and Jack, and saw that they sensed the same thing. We all looked at Gregor, but he only smiled.

"It is the nature of the Dark's biotech in our bloodstreams, gentlemen," said Gregor. "We are essentially network nodes, and here, there are so many more potential incoming connections."

"What are you talking about?" said Vance.

"A change in sensation, sir," said Jack. "The Darksiders haven't come any closer, but the sense of both Gregor and the major crystal have changed."

"That going to be a problem?" said Vance. The APC creaked as it started to climb the first hill.

"Don't know, sir," said Jack. "Mr. Gregor."

"I don't believe so," said Gregor. "As I told the young men, it is to be expected. I have never done this before, after all."

The captain said something unflattering under his breath, shook his head, and kept driving.

About two minutes later the APCs had pulled up in a ring along the top of the hill with the crystal, encircling the corpse-flower and the floating crystal.

"Status," said Vance.

"The Darksiders are moving from the mushroom forest, sir," said Jack. "Think they're still eleven minutes away. Maybe a little more or less."

"Then let's do this," said Vance, pushing out of his seat. "Let's go." He tapped his mike. "The Listeners, Gregor, and I are heading out. Everyone else is to stay in their vehicles and maintain watch on the surrounding countryside. Report at the first sign of trouble."

A chorus of acknowledgements went over the radio, and we followed Vance out of the APC, escorting Gregor. We stopped a few feet from the corpse-flower and its floating crystal, and I felt the familiar pressure inside my skull. I also felt a new pressure from the major crystal in the box. I had the feeling the major crystal was trying to talk to the smaller one, though I didn't know what message it was trying to send. To shut down? That the war was over?

"The crystal, if you please, Corporal Rigger," said Gregor, holding out one bony hand. "It is time for us to make history today."

Rigger looked at the captain, grunted, and opened the strongbox. He set it down and drew out the crystal, wincing a little as he touched it. White light flashed and flickered within its black facets. With both hands, he handed it to Gregor. The old man lifted the crystal one-handed, gazing into its facets, a strange look of exultation going over his lined face.

The major crystal's sense changed. So did Gregor's sense. Suddenly the two of them felt like a single entity of the Dark.

"Hello," murmured Gregor, "harlot."

I blinked. Harlot? Had he just called the crystal a harlot? That made no sense. It was such a weirdly specific insult. And why insult the crystal? The thing might have been intelligent, but it was so far from the human version of intelligence that attempting to insult it would be like shouting at a tree.

Gregor walked forward, holding the major crystal before him and gazing into its depths, his expression intent and sharp. He stopped a yard from the lesser crystal, the major crystal starting to flash in his grasp. Despite the weight of the thing, he held it before him one-handed, his arm rock-solid.

The lesser crystal began to flash as well, and I realized that the major crystal and the lesser crystal were now flashing in perfect sync. A strange sensation went through my head, and I realized that the sense of the Darksiders approaching us from the giant mushrooms had changed. They felt… different. They felt like…

I blinked.

They felt a little like Gregor, like his presence had copied itself into the approaching Darksiders.

I didn't think he was doing anything to the gates.

Rigger stepped forward, scowling. Jack started to point his weapon at Gregor, and I followed suit.

"What is it?" said Vance. "What's he doing?"

"I don't know, sir," I said. "But it's not affecting the gates."

"Gregor!" shouted Vance. "What are you doing?"

"Do not interrupt me," said Gregor. "This is delicate work. Yes… almost there. You will obey me, harlot. You will obey me!"

The sense of Gregor in the approaching Darksiders intensified, and with a horrified shock I realized what was happening.

"He's taking control of them," I said. "He might be able to close the gates, but he didn't come here to do that. I think he's trying to take control of the Dark!"

Gregor whirled to face us, the major crystal clenched in his left hand, his withered lips pulled back from his yellowed teeth in a snarl. His eyes had turned black, like the eyes of the converted zombies, his veins turning black beneath his papery skin. He looked like one of the zombies, but unlike the zombies, his expression had not gone slack, and was filled with gloating malice.

The conversion weapons joined humans to the Dark's hive mind.

I suspected that Gregor had just done the opposite.

"Kill him!" said Vance, raising his own weapon.

We started shooting, but even before we pulled the triggers on our weapons, the major crystal glowed with white light. A dome of translucent white light exploded out from the crystal and swept across the hilltop, surrounding Gregor. Our bullets hit the dome and rebounded as if they had hit concrete.

The expanding dome hit me across the body, and I flew backwards and struck the APC behind me. My head bounced off the armored vehicle, and I felt the force of the impact even through my helmet.

Things got woozy, and I slid to the ground.

I think I blacked out for a moment.

When I came to, things were not going well.

I heard the steady roar of machine gun fire, and Vance barking orders. I felt the presence of Gregor and the major crystal nearby, and I also felt the presence of thousands upon thousands of copies of Gregor approaching from the sky. That didn't make sense. Gregor couldn't copy himself.

Then my eyes opened wider and I tried to stand up.

The dome of light filled most of the hilltop, enclosing Gregor and both crystals. All the APCs had opened up with the machine guns, their bullets rebounding from the dome.

"Cease fire!" said Vance.

"Explosives, sir?" said Jack.

"Won't do any good," said Vance. "If that barrier can absorb the kinetic force of six machine guns at once, an explosion won't help us."

"It is useless."

It was Gregor's voice, and I heard him speaking through the dome… but I also heard his voice booming over the hills, coming from the direction of the mushroom forest. It sounded like his voice had been repeated thousands and thousands of times. I couldn't understand it, but then I realized the source.

The thousands of Darksiders flying towards us were using their mouthparts in unison to simulate Gregor's voice.

"You cannot stop me any longer," said the hellish chorus. "I found the secret to controlling the Dark. I shall inaugurate a new age of global unity, and I shall forge the new world order. There will be no more classes, no more religions, no more nations. All shall be one, and anything that opposes the new order will be destroyed." I heard the smirk in his voice. "Beginning, I think, with Black Division and Castle Base."

"Sir, we've got to get out of here," said a soldier I didn't recognize. "I can see Darksiders approaching. There must be thousands of them."

"Tens of thousands," said Gregor and his chorus.

"We leave now, we're dead," snapped Vance. "He'll control the Dark, and he'll coordinate them against us. We've only been beating them because they don't understand us and they don't understand how to fight us. Gregor does. Get ready to blow the APCs. Every single explosive we have. Maybe that will overload this force field of his."

Gregor's scornful laughter answered him.

I had to help them. I had to stand up. I tried to stand, but a wave of dizziness overwhelmed me. I slumped back against the APC, blinking. The glow from the dome dazzled my eyes, but I saw Gregor's dark shape within it. I saw the soldiers hurrying to their APCs, preparing to explode them, even though they knew they wouldn't be able to get back to the gate on foot in time. I turned my head, saw Rigger and Jack hurrying behind Vance as the captain barked orders.

Maggie crouched next to me, gazing at me with a quizzical expression.

"Maggie?" I croaked.

She blinked. "This word-symbol is not known to me."

"My sister," I said.

"Ah," said Maggie.

"But you're not my sister," I said. "She's back at Castle Base. You're… you're the major crystal, aren't you? Talking to me inside my head."

"I am not," said Maggie. "What your senses currently experience is an interface constructed from your memories and capable of communicating via the primitive word-symbols that underlie your cognitive processes. This only utilizes the millionth part of my capacity, but it is the only channel of communication available."

I blinked, trying to think through the pain in the back of my head. Interface. Maggie, the real Maggie, had talked about interfaces on her computers. So I knew that an interface was a program that communicated between the user and the computer. Which meant…

I blinked again, my eyes gummy.

Harlot. Gregor had called the crystal a harlot. But that was such an oddly specific insult.

A memory flickered through my sluggish brain. He had called his mother a harlot when I had first met him, when he had decided to amuse himself by telling me his life story.

Did that mean he saw his mother the way that I now saw Maggie? Was he telling the phantasm of his mother what to do?

Had he constructed an interface for controlling the major crystal out of the memories of his mother?

"Interface," I said. "Gregor can see his mother, can't he? That's how he's controlling the crystal. He's telling his mother what to do."

"There is a concurrent user session," said Maggie. "The human you identify as Mikhail Gregor has initiated a command session. His interface is constructed of the memories of his female progenitor."

"But you're the interface too," I said. "I can tell you what to do. I can issue you commands, right?"

"Why do you wish to issue commands?" said Maggie, turning her flat, unblinking gaze toward me.

"Because," I said, groping for words. "Because… because Gregor's going to use you to take over the world. He'll kill a lot of people with you. He'll keep the war going." The memory of our previous conversation flashed through my mind. "Because he wants to keep the war going. I want to end the war. You told me the war is over. This has to stop. I want it to stop."

Maggie considered me for a moment. "This is an acceptable user parameter. You may attempt to issue commands."

"Okay," I said. "Shut it off. Whatever Gregor is doing to control the Dark. Shut it off."

"I can't do that," said Maggie.

"Why not?" I said.

"The human called Gregor has physical access to the crystal, which authorizes a higher level of access," said Maggie. "Priority will be given to his commands due to physical proximity."

That meant I had to get the crystal away from him. Or someone had to get the crystal away from him. But that meant getting through the force dome he had somehow created around himself.

"The force field," I said. "Can you take it down?"

"The defensive countermeasures have been activated," said Maggie. "They are designed to block anyone outside the hive mind from entering its area of influence. The defensive countermeasures can only be countermanded by the issuer of the command."

I grimaced. That meant only Gregor could take down the force field. "Can anything penetrate it?"

"No technology available on your planet can overwhelm the defensive countermeasure," said Maggie.

"Get ready to move!" shouted Vance. "Rigger, Walter, get Kane if he's still alive."

No, we couldn't leave now. I was so close. I just had to think of something…

"Wait," I said. "You said only members of the hive mind can pass the force field."

"This is accurate," said Maggie.

"I'm part of the hive mind, sort of," I said, heaving myself to my feet. The hilltop spun around me. I had to get to the dome. Fortunately, it was only a few yards away. I started forward, weaving a bit as I did.

"Come on, Roland, it's time to go," said Jack, Rigger jogging behind him.

"No," I said. "The dome. I can get through the dome."

Jack walked through Maggie like she wasn't there. I suppose she wasn't. "We've got to go. We…"

I couldn't find the words to argue. I shouted and threw myself forward, and slammed into the curve of the dome. That hurt. It felt like running into a concrete wall. For an instant, nothing happened, and then the dome became… soft, like pushing at plastic wrap.

Then I heard a popping sound, and I was through.

I stumbled towards Gregor. He stood still holding the crystal, gazing at it with a frown. Maggie stood next to him, and I hadn't seen her move. Or maybe the interface appeared when I happened to think about the crystal.

I charged at Gregor. At least, I tried to charge at Gregor. Except I had a concussion, and my brain and reflexes weren't working at all well. My charge turned into sort of a drunken, staggering wobble, and I almost spun around and fell over. Gregor looked at me in astonishment, his black eyes widening, and belatedly I remembered that I had a gun. Except I had dropped my carbine, but I still had a pistol holstered at my belt.

In the time it took me to remember that, Gregor sprang forward with alarming quickness, the major crystal drawn back. I thought he would shoot energy from it, or a laser, or something like that.

Instead, he whacked me upside the head with it.

In addition to opening portals through space-time, the crystal made one heck of a blunt object.

Another explosion of pain went through my head, and I spun and fell and landed on my back. Gregor drew back the crystal to hit me again, then his eyes strayed to my belt and he snatched the pistol from my holster. I thought he would say something gloating or threatening, but then I remembered that he had started his career as a KGB officer and he wouldn't screw around when his life was in danger.

He raised the pistol to point at my face, and I saw my death in his hand.

Then his eyes widened again, and he changed his angle and started shooting. I heard Rigger bellow in rage, and then Mikhail Gregor's face and chest exploded from the impact of multiple high-caliber rounds. He staggered and collapsed dead to the ground, the major crystal rolling away from his hand.

I heard Rigger start cursing.

The force dome winked out of existence, and my sense of the Dark changed somehow, losing the texture of Gregor's mind.

"You're hit," said Jack. "It's not bad, though. Clean through the arm. Didn't hit the bone or the blood vessel."

Rigger bellowed another curse. "Two years! Two and a half years I've been fighting the Dark, and I never got wounded once! Then I get shot by a withered old chipmunk!"

There was a gunshot, and Gregor's corpse jerked again.

"Don't waste the ammo," snapped Jack. "He's dead."

"Right," grumbled Rigger.

I looked up and saw Jack and Rigger standing over me. Rigger was grabbing his left arm. For a man who had just been shot, he looked more angry than in pain. Like someone had just insulted his mother or something.

"Roland," said Jack. "You okay?"

"Yeah," I managed to say. I looked over and saw Maggie standing near the crystal. "No."

"Killing the previous user," said Maggie, "activated the defensive protocols. All available drones of all classes are coming here at maximum possible speed."

"What happened?" said Vance, stepping next to Jack and Rigger.

I forced myself to sit up, and I grabbed the crystal that Gregor had dropped.

"We've got to go," I said. "Captain Vance. I can talk to the crystal. That's what Gregor was doing. But we've got to take the lesser crystal and go."

"Can't," said Vance, pointing.

I saw that the lesser crystal had generated its own force dome, shielding itself from any attack.

"This defensive protocol is hardwired and cannot be countermanded," said Maggie. "Nor will it permit any members of the hive mind to contravene it."

"Ah," I said. "Sir, the crystal says we can't shut down the force dome."

"But you can talk to the crystal?" said Vance.

"Yes, sir," I said. "Like Gregor could. Well, not like Gregor. I can't take over the Dark the way he did. The crystal says they're all coming to kill us."

Vance rubbed his face. "I'm taking orders from talking crystals, and we can't close that scout gate. Okay, we've got to get Corporal Kane back to Earth and Castle Base. If he can talk to the crystal, the scientists can figure out what to do with him. He's got to get away, regardless of the cost."

Regardless of the cost? That meant Vance and the others would try to hold the gate against thousands of Darksiders so I could get away. They couldn't, and they would get killed.

I started to protest, but Jack and Rigger hauled me toward one of the APCs. Rigger's arm was wounded, but it didn't seem to slow him down. I all but collapsed into the seat, my head spinning, my stomach churning, the major crystal clutched in my lap. Head injuries aren't fun, but I had to think of something. Bull and Captain Howard and Sergeant Mendez and all their company had died at Spokane, and I had survived. It was about to happen again.

"Maggie," I said.

"Who?" Rigger said.

"His sister. He's delirious," said Jack.

"No, I'm not," I said, staring at where Maggie leaned against the wall of the APC. "The gate. Can I command you to close the gate?"

"The gate may not be closed from this side," said Maggie.

"But what about the other side?" I said.

"Roland? Who are you talking to?" said Jack.

"Go!" I heard Vance say.

"What about the other side?" I said.

"An override may be issued from there," said Maggie.

"Captain!" I said. "Captain Vance." My voice sounded slurred. "We've got to get through the gate. We've got to get through the gate as soon as possible."

"I know," said Vance, and I heard the APC's motor surge to full power. "Go!"

It was a jouncing, bouncing ride through the hills back to the gate at full speed, and I sensed the Dark closing in around us. The roar of machine gun fire filled my ears, followed by Vance barking orders over the radio and the explosion of multiple Javelin rounds. The presence of the gate grew sharper and harder, and then we were through, the light changing to normal sunlight.

The presence of the furious Dark followed us.

"All right," said Jack. "We've got to get Kane and the crystal back to base. Let's…"

"Now!" I screamed at Maggie. "Close it, close it, close it."

"Override issued," said Maggie.

For the next minute, it was only chaos, with the roar of machine guns and the buzz of the attacking Darksiders, Vance shouting orders over the radio and Sergeant Hobb responding.

Then silence fell.

"Sir," said Sergeant Hobb. "The gate… the gate's just gone. It just disappeared. You didn't bring back the transductor, did you?"

"No," said Vance, twisting in his seat to look at me.

So did Rigger, Jack, and everyone else in the APC, and Rigger was busy putting a field dressing on his wound.

I tried to smile. "I asked the crystal to close the gate, and it did."

"How… how did you get the crystal to do that?" said Vance, as astonished as I had ever seen him.

"We both want the same thing, sir," I said. "We both want the war to be over."

Chapter 12

Diaspora

I had thought my first three years in Black Division were busy.

The five years after the death of Mikhail Gregor were just insane.

Once we got back to Castle Base and I got out of the infirmary (again), I spent even more quality time with the Division's scientists and intelligence officers. Apparently, my ability to talk to the crystal was a big deal, and rewrote a bunch of scientific theories. I suspect they would have kept me down there for the rest of my life, but General Culver had another use for me.

I could tell the major transductor crystal to close gates, and we had a lot of gates to close.

I couldn't do it by remote control, and I had to be within visual range to close the gate, but it was a lot easier than venturing to the other side to shut down the gate. Six months after Gregor died during his failed bid for tyrannical godhood, we retook Seattle, and we claimed another major crystal from the Seattle gate. By then, the scientists had figured out just how the Listeners could communicate with the crystals, so Major Randolph got to be the second Listener equipped with a crystal. Evidently for him the crystal's interface took the form of his wife, which alarmed his actual wife a little.

By the end of the first year, we had five Listeners equipped with crystals, and the liberation of the former United States proceeded apace. We soon had cleared the former U.S. of gates, and Randolph, Jack, Rigger, and I spent a lot of time flying overseas to visit allies of Black Division and help them close their gates. In a single year, I visited every single continent except Antarctica.

Two and a half years after that, the war was basically over. There were still occasional Darksider incursions, but we dealt with them quickly.

We had won.

There were a lot of political changes, but to be honest I didn't pay much attention to them. General Culver resigned to serve as the first president of the new nation of Pacifica, though the various parts of the eastern U.S. that had come through intact preferred to rule themselves. Black Division spent some time hunting down the surviving members of the Global Defense Committee, putting them on trial for crimes against humanity, and then executing them. Sergeant Hobb was especially pleased when the man who had invented his ex-wife's favorite smartphone game was executed for his role in the GDC, though he probably wasn't pleased for the right reasons.

Jack was really excited about the constitution of Pacifica. Apparently only men who had honorably completed a term of military service and married women who had borne one or more children were allowed to vote (I guess the General had included that to keep the Mormons happy). Jack thought that would solve a lot of the social and political problems the old U.S. had endured.

I dunno. I'm not an optimist. I'm too much my father's son for that, and after Jack got elected to the Assembly, he explained it all to me. But I seemed to hear my father's voice pointing out all the things that could go wrong.

At least the interface had appeared to me as Maggie instead of my father. That would have been too weird.

I did see less of Maggie once she got married, I'm afraid to say, but that's only natural. A couple of weeks after her eighteenth birthday, an infantryman named Kyle Holmberg nervously approached me and asked for permission to marry Maggie, since I was the closest thing to her father. I looked up Holmberg's service record and said it was fine by me, and I joked that if he treated her badly, I would feed him to the Dark.

That was a joke, of course. If he treated her badly, I would just shoot him and have Rigger help me bury the body in the desert.

I think he believed me. Certainly Maggie was happy with him. They got married and the first baby came a year later, named after Dad. I don't know how Daniel Kane would have thought of little Daniel Holmberg, but I think he would have approved. Maybe a grandbaby would even have made him crack a smile.

Jack got married, too, to some blond woman who smiled a lot and liked being an Assemblyman's wife, and even Rigger had a steady girlfriend. Me, though… no. I had seen too much. I had seen other worlds, and I wanted to see more of them.

The crystal showed me how.

After the war more or less ended, I remained with Black Division, though I basically worked with the scientists as a translator, putting questions to the major transductor crystal and seeing how it answered. We couldn't use it to open new gates, and the only thing we ever figured out how to make it do was to close gates. But the crystal would respond to any questions I posed to it, kind of like an alien version of a search engine, though the answers were always cryptic.

Then one of the scientists had the bright idea of posing the questions to the crystal in mathematical form… which the crystal then answered in mathematical format.

I don't think I had ever seen anyone so excited as those scientists.

The first set of equations that the crystal solved for us allowed the creation of the first fusion reactor. I didn't understand it at the time, since I thought it was just a fancy nuclear plant, but that was a big deal.

Then the scientists started asking about specific equations by scientists with names like Hendrik Casimir and van der Waal and some guy named Alcubierre. That last one was an even bigger deal than the fusion plant. When the crystal produced the results of some of those equations, the scientists almost had a spontaneous celebration right there in the laboratory. One of them actually fainted.

Eventually, they bothered to explain the cause of the excitement to me.

Using the equations from the crystal, they could build a hyperdrive. An actual, working hyperdrive that through some trick of physics let a ship travel way faster than the speed of light. And not in a hundred years or some distant future, but they could build it here and now. President Culver authorized the funds for the program, and the military of Pacifica started building its first hyperdrive-capable starship.

I requested permission to join the exploration program, and the President personally approved it in his role as commander of the armed forces.

"You know," Jack told me at the reception at the legislature, "I don't want to leave, but I'm jealous of you."

I had been invited to the official start of the project at Pacifica's capital, which for reasons of political compromise was located in Grand Junction, Colorado. President Culver hosted the party. A lot of veterans were there, most of whom I knew. Maggie and Kyle and their kids had come as well. Even Rigger and his girlfriend had come, though I suspect they mostly wanted the free food and drink.

"Alpha Centauri first," I said. "Nine days to get there. The chief scientist thinks they'll even be able to work out the equation for artificial gravity by then."

"I wouldn't want to leave," said Jack, "but... that will be something, won't it? The first one to see a thousand different worlds."

"A thousand worlds," said Rigger around a mouthful of egg rolls.

"Eh?" I said.

"See, maybe that's what they'll call it," said Rigger. "They keep calling it the galaxy or unexplored space or whatever. Maybe they'll call it the Thousand Worlds someday."

"Heck of a thought," I said.

"Eh," said Rigger. "Too bad old Gregor didn't live to see it." He guffawed. "He would have been ticked."

"Yeah," I said.

Jack snorted. "You're turning into a philosopher in your old age, Nate. Gregor wanted to turn Earth into a prison that he and his friends could rule for themselves. Instead, he accidentally gave humanity a way to the stars."

"Eh," said Rigger. "Too poetic for me. I'm just glad I got to shoot him myself."

"The thousand worlds," I said, mulling the thought over.

I did like the thought of that. One thousand worlds, and I wanted to see as many of them as I could before I died.

It was time to get started.